—

'I need to get over the hurt.' Tasha was trying her hardest to keep this conversation grounded. 'Like you. You're improving every day.'

'I'm not talking about physical hurt. It's the other hurt that stays with us. Watching my father break my mother's heart... Watching your husband betray you... Watching Emily die...' And then he stopped.

There was a long, long silence. She couldn't break it. She didn't know how.

And then... 'Tasha, I'd really like to kiss you.'

This was a bad idea. Her head knew it, but somehow tonight she'd passed the point where her head was in control.

The night. The pain she'd just tried to express. His pain.

Tom...

She'd never spoken to anyone as she'd just spoken to Tom. She tried to hide her pain, not put it out there for anyone to see.

Only this wasn't *anyone*.

Tom was her friend. He was the man she'd gone to when she was in trouble. He was a colleague, someone who'd helped her, and she could help him back. A man who'd suffered a cerebral bleed.

He was all of those things, but above all he was Tom.

Dear Reader,

I've recently moved to a small coastal village where the sand squishes between my toes, where the waves are a gentle background murmur and where I lie in bed at night and listen to the foghorns of ships as they head off into the unknown. And as I get to know my new home I'm realising that many of its residents are here for a reason. This place can be wild, windswept and awe-inspiring...or it can be calm and breathtakingly beautiful. Either way, it seems a place for healing.

The thought of such healing is what's inspired *Falling for Her Wounded Hero*. My heroine has lost her baby, and my hero has suffered life-changing injuries in a surfing accident. They're both doctors, but they can't heal themselves. Not alone.

But for the last few months my dog and I have walked my beach, over and over, until I've worked out how their strength, their hope, their love and their laughter, combined with the support of their wonderful seaside community, can finally let them find their future.

Enjoy,

Marion Lennox

FALLING FOR HER WOUNDED HERO

BY
MARION LENNOX

First published in Great Britain 2017
By Mills & Boon, an imprint of HarperCollins*Publishers*
1 London Bridge Street, London, SE1 9GF

Large Print edition 2017

© 2017 Marion Lennox

ISBN: 978-0-263-06707-1

Our policy is to use papers that are natural, renewable and recyclable products and made from wood grown in sustainable forests. The logging and manufacturing processes conform to the legal environmental regulations of the country of origin.

Printed and bound in Great Britain
by CPI Antony Rowe, Chippenham, Wiltshire

3390555x

Marion Lennox has written over a hundred romance novels, and is published in over a hundred countries and thirty languages. Her international awards include the prestigious RITA® Award (twice) and the *RT Book Reviews* Career Achievement award for 'a body of work which makes us laugh and teaches us about love'. Marion adores her family, her kayak, her dog and lying on the beach with a book someone else has written. Heaven!

Books by Marion Lennox

Mills & Boon Medical Romance

Wildfire Island Docs

Saving Maddie's Baby
A Child to Open Their Hearts

Meant-to-Be Family
From Christmas to Forever?

Mills & Boon Cherish

His Cinderella Heiress
Stepping into the Prince's World

Visit the Author Profile page
at millsandboon.co.uk for more titles.

CHAPTER ONE

THE SURF OUTSIDE his surgery window was calling like a siren's song. Sunlit waves were rolling in with perfect symmetry. Dr Tom Blake had been watching them between patients, crossing his fingers that his list for the afternoon stayed short.

It did. Cray Point was a small town tucked away on a peninsula on Australia's south-east coast, and almost without exception its residents loved the ocean. On a day like this, only the most urgent medical problems replaced the call of the surf.

Which meant Tom could surf, too.

'That's it,' he called to his receptionist as he closed his last patient file. 'We're out of here.'

'One more,' Rhonda called back. 'A last-minute booking. Mrs Tasha Raymond's here to see you.'

Tasha Raymond.

A tourist? Something easy, he hoped, and headed out to usher her in.

And stopped.

The woman was sitting at the far side of his waiting room. She was close to thirty, he thought, and very pregnant. She had the exhausted and shadowed look he sometimes saw when pregnant women had too much to cope with—toddlers at home, too many work commitments, or a deep unhappiness at the pregnancy itself.

She was small, five four or five, and fair skinned, with brown curls caught into an unruly knot. She was wearing maternity jeans and an enormous windcheater. The shadows under her eyes suggested she hadn't slept for days.

And he knew her. Tasha Raymond? He'd met her as Tasha Blake.

'Tasha,' he said, and she managed a smile and struggled to rise.

'Tom. I didn't think you'd recognise me.'

Fair point. Tasha was his half-brother's widow but he'd only met her once, at Paul's funeral four years ago.

He'd attended because he'd thought he should, not because he'd thought he was wanted. His stepmother had made it clear she'd prefer it if he stayed away. He'd gone, though, and had stayed in the background, and then one of Paul's climbing mates who knew the family background had decided to intervene and introduce him.

'Tom, I doubt if you've met Tasha. Did you know Tasha and Paul were married?'

The news that Paul had died trying to scale Everest had come as no huge surprise. Paul had spent his life moving from one adventure to another, taking bigger and bigger risks along the way. The knowledge that he'd found time to marry had been a bigger shock.

But the slight figure surrounded by Paul's climbing friends had seemed almost a ghost. He'd told her how sorry he was, but he'd only had time for few perfunctory words.

For of course his stepmother had moved in. Afterwards he'd never been able to figure if her contempt was only for him, or if it had included Tasha. Tasha had been a pale figure huddled into someone else's greatcoat to protect her from the icy winds at the graveside—and maybe also from her mother-in-law?

There'd seemed little point in pursuing the acquaintance, though. And after giving his condolences he'd left.

Four years ago.

Why was her face etched on his memory? Why was recognition so instant?

The notes in his hand said she was Tasha Raymond. She was obviously pregnant. Had she remarried? Four years was time to have moved on.

Rhonda was looking from Tom to Tasha with bright interest. Rhonda was the world's worst gossip—well, maybe apart from her twin sister. Tom employed them both. Rhonda was his receptionist and Hilda was his housekeeper. The widowed, middle-aged sisters were excellent at their jobs but to say they were nosy was an understatement.

'I can manage from here, Rhonda,' he told her, smiling at Tasha with what he hoped was a brisk, professional nod. 'You can go.'

'Oh, but Mrs Raymond—'

'Mrs Raymond is my late half-brother's widow,' he told her. He might as well. Rhonda would have asked Tasha to fill in a patient form and she'd have probably figured her history before he had. 'I imagine she's here on family business. There's no need for you to stay.'

who pushed his physical limits? Who thought risks were fun?

She couldn't help it. She shuddered.

She was here because she needed him. Needing another Blake? The thought made her feel ill.

'Tasha,' he said softly, and his attention was all on her. 'How can I help?'

It would have been a shock to see her, she thought. It had been a surprise to meet him at Paul's funeral. This man and Paul had never been permitted to be brothers.

'My mother would disown me if she ever caught me talking to that side of the family,' Paul had told her. 'Which always seemed a shame. When I was a kid my father took me on a holiday, supposedly just father and son. Unbeknown to my mother, he invited my half-brother, too. Tom's four years older than me and I thought he was cool. Kind, too, to a kid who trailed after him. But of course Mum found out and hit the roof and as a kid I never saw him again. We met a couple of times later on with Dad, but then we lost touch. In an odd way, though, it's always seemed like I have a brother. If anything happened to me, Tasha, I reckon you could go to him.'

If anything happened to him. Like being crushed by tons of ice on Everest.

She hadn't needed Tom then, though, and she'd made a vow. She'd never *need* anyone again. Not like she'd needed her parents or thought she'd needed Paul. Paul had made her world crumble even before he'd been killed.

So what was she doing now, asking for help from another Blake? Paul and his father had both been charming, undependable womanisers. Why should this man be different?

Because she needed him? Because she'd taken yet another risk and failed.

Her last risk.

'Tasha?' Tom's voice was still gentle, that of a concerned family doctor. Maybe that was the way to go, she thought. She could talk to him as one medic to another.

Only she didn't feel like a medic. She felt like a terrified single mum who'd just heard the worst of news.

'Tea,' Tom was saying, suddenly brisk, and his hands were on her shoulders and he was propelling her back into her seat. 'You look exhausted. I'm thinking tea with lots of sugar and then take your time and tell me all.'

'I should have booked for a long consultation,' she managed, trying to joke. 'I only booked for standard. You'll be out of pocket.'

'Do you think I'd charge?' His voice was suddenly strained but he had his back to her, putting on the kettle at the little sink behind Rhonda's desk. 'You're family.'

Family. She stared blankly at his broad back, at the tanned and muscled arms emerging from his crisp, white short-sleeved shirt, at the stethoscope dangling casually from his back pocket.

He oozed competence. He oozed caring.

He was a family doctor. This was what he did. There was no reason for her to want to well up and demand a hug and turn his shoulder into a sodden mess just because he'd said the word 'family'.

She wouldn't.

But she needed him and the very thought had her terrified.

So she sat on, silent, trying to keep her thoughts in check.

Tom spent time making tea, checking how she had it, measuring sugar, stirring for maybe longer than it needed, as if he sensed she needed time to get herself together. By the time he set the mug into her cupped hands and tugged a chair up before her so he could sit down and face her, she had the stupid tears at bay again. She was under control—or as under control as she could be after the appalling news of two days ago.

'Now.' Tom was smiling at her, his very best patient-reassuring smile, a smile she recognised as one she'd practised as a new doctor. Family or not, she was clearly in the category of new client who may or may not have something diabolical going on.

There was a box of tissues on the side bench. He swiped it surreptitiously forward—or not so surreptitiously as she noticed and she even managed a smile.

'I won't cry on you.'

'You're very welcome to cry if you want. I wouldn't have minded it you'd cried on me four years ago. That one meeting and then you were gone...'

'To England,' she told him. 'I couldn't stay here. Paul's mother blamed—'

'Paul's mother is a vituperative cow,' he said solidly, and Tasha thought of Deidre and thought she couldn't have put it better herself.

'She thought I should have stopped Paul trying to climb.'

'No one could ever stop Paul doing what he wanted to do.'

'You knew him?'

'Not much. My mum was happy for me to meet Paul but Paul's mother…not. When Dad moved on from Deidre as well, it made things even more complicated. Dad was a serial womaniser. My mum coped okay—she got on with her life—but Deidre stayed bitter. She fought Dad's access to Paul every inch of the way. Dad cared about both Paul and me, but with Paul he ended up sidelined. As we got older Paul and I used to meet a bit. We'd have a drink with Dad occasionally, but after Dad's death we lost touch. Tasha, you need to drink.'

'What…?'

He took her cupped hands in his and propelled the mug to her lips. 'Tea. Drink.'

She drank and was vaguely surprised by how good it tasted. When had she last had tea?

Come to think if it, when had she last eaten?

Great. Collapsing would help no one.

Neither would coming here. She should face this herself.

She couldn't. She needed... Tom.

'So tell me why you're here?' he asked.

She'd come this far but she didn't want to tell him. She didn't want to tell anyone.

Telling people made it real. It couldn't be real. It had to be a nightmare.

'Tasha, spill,' Tom said, in that gentle voice that did something to her insides. It made things settle. It made the battering ram in her heart cease for a moment.

Though of course it started up again. Some things were inescapable.

'My baby...' she started, and Tom sat back a little and eyed her bulge.

'Close to term?'

'I'm due to deliver next week.'

He nodded, as if it was entirely sensible that a close-to-term pregnant woman had decided to drive to Cray Point just to see him.

She should keep talking.

She couldn't.

'Do you have a partner?' he asked tentatively when she couldn't figure what to say next. 'Is the baby's dad around?'

And finally she found the strength to make her voice work. 'The baby's father is Paul.'

'Paul...'

'He left sperm,' she managed. She'd started. She had to find the strength to continue. 'That last climb... I was so angry with him for going. There'd been two landslides on Everest, major ones. The Sherpas were pulling out for the season, as were most of the climbers, but he still insisted on going. Then he came home that last night before he left, laughing. "I've got it sorted, babe," he told me. "I've been to the IVF place and left sperm. It's all paid for, stored for years. If worst comes to worst you can have a little me to take my place."'

She paused, searching for the words to go on. 'I think it was a joke,' she said. 'Maybe he thought it'd make me laugh. Or maybe he was serious—I have no way of telling. But I knew... I waved goodbye to him and somehow I knew that I'd never see him again.'

She tilted her chin, meeting his look head on. 'I was almost too angry to go to his funeral,' she told him. 'It was such a stupid, stupid waste. And then Deidre was in my face, blaming me, making nasty phone calls, even turning up at work to yell at me. So I left for England. You know I'm a doctor, too? I took a job in the emergency department in a good London hospital and I decided I'd put Paul behind me. Only then...then I sort of fell in a heap.'

Tasha shrugged. How to explain the wall of despair that had hit her? The knowledge that her marriage to Paul had been a farce. That her judgement was so far off...

She remembered waking one morning and thinking she was never going to trust again, and the thought had been followed by emptiness. If she couldn't trust again, that excluded her from having a family. A baby. The thought had been almost overwhelming.

'So you decided to use the sperm,' Tom said, as if he was following her thoughts, and she felt a surge of anger that was pretty much directed at her naïve self.

'Why not?' she flashed. 'Paul left it to me in his will. I could bring our baby up knowing the good things about Paul, feeling like it knew its dad. It seemed better—safer—than using an unknown donor, so I decided I'd be brave enough to try.'

And then she hugged her swollen belly, and the tears at last welled over.

'I wanted this baby,' she whispered. 'I wanted her so much...'

Wanted. Past tense. The word was like a knife to her heart. She heard it and tried to change it.

'I want her,' she said, and her voice broke on a sob, but there was no changing what the scans had shown.

And Tom leaned forward and put his hands over hers, so there were four hands cupped over her belly.

'Has your baby died, Tasha?'

And there it was, out there in all its horror. But it couldn't be real. Please…

'Not yet,' she managed, and his grip on her hands tightened. I wonder if this is the way he treats all his patients, she thought, in some weird abstracted part of her brain that had space for those things. He was good. He was intuitive, empathic, caring. He'd be a good family doctor.

A good friend?

'If anything happened to me, Tasha, I reckon you could go to him.'

Paul had been right, she thought. For just about the only time in his life, Paul had been right.

Oh, but laying this on him…

And he was a Blake. He even looked like his brother.

'Tell me,' he said, and it was an order, calm and

sure, a direction she had to follow no matter how she was feeling. And she took a deep breath because this was what she'd come for. She had no choice but to continue.

'My baby's a girl,' she whispered. 'Emily. I've named her Emily after my grandma. I had to come back to Australia to access Paul's sperm. I'm Australian and I have Aussie health insurance so I stayed here during my pregnancy. I've been doing locums. Everything was fine until the last ultrasound. And they picked it up. She has hypoplastic left heart syndrome. The left side of her heart hasn't developed. That...that's bad enough but I thought...well, the literature says there's hope and there are good people in Melbourne. With the Norwood procedure there's a good chance of long-term survival. I hoped. But two days ago I went for my last visit to the cardiologist before delivery and the ultrasound's showing an atrial septal defect as well. And more. Nothing's right. Everything's wrong. While she's in utero, she doesn't need her heart to pump her lungs, so she's okay, but as soon as she's born...'

She took a deep breath. 'As soon as she's born the problems will start. The cardiologist says I need to wait as long as possible before delivery

so she's strong enough to face the faint possibil-
ity of surgery, but I'm not to hope for miracles.
He says she'll live for a little while but it'll be
days. Or less. The defect is so great...'

Strangely her voice was working okay. Strangely
the words didn't cut out. It was like the medical
side of her was kicking in, giving her some kind
of armour against the pain. Or maybe it was simply that the pain was so unbearable that her body
had thrown up armour of its own.

Tom's face had stilled. He'd be taking it in,
she thought, like a good doctor, taking his time
to assess, to figure what to say, to think of what
might be the most helpful thing to say.

There wasn't anything to say. There just...
wasn't.

Hypoplastic left heart syndrome...

He'd never seen a case but he'd read of it. He'd
read of the Norwood procedure, a radical surgical technique giving hope to such babies, but
with an atrial septal defect as well...

His hands were still gripping Tasha's. They
were resting against the bulge that was her baby,
and he felt a faint movement. A kick...

In cases like this there usually weren't any

outward signs during pregnancy. A foetus only needed one ventricle. It didn't use its lungs to get oxygen to the body, so while it was in utero there was nothing wrong.

If the experts were right, Tasha was carrying a seemingly healthy baby, a little girl who'd only survive for days after she was born.

This woman was a doctor. She'd have gone down every path. Her face said she had, and she'd been hit by a wall at every turn.

'Transplant?' he said, still holding her hands, and he thought maybe it was for him as well as for her. He had a sudden vision of his half-brother as a child, a tousled-haired wild child, rebellious even as a kid. A bright kid who'd tumbled from scrape to scrape. Paul had done medicine, too. Their father had been a doctor so maybe that's why it had appealed to both of them, but the moment Paul had graduated he'd been off overseas. He'd helped out in some of the wildest places. He'd been a risk taker.

And now he was dead and his baby was facing the biggest risk of all. Being born.

A transplant? Without research it sounded the only hope.

'You must know the odds,' Tasha said flatly, echoing his thoughts.

He did. To find a suitable donor in time... To keep this little one alive until they found one, and then to have her fight the odds and survive...

He glanced up at Tasha's ravaged face and he thought, *Where are your friends? Where are your family? Why are you here alone?*

And something inside him twisted.

He'd been a family doctor for ten years now. He loved the work. He loved this little community and when his patients were ill he couldn't help but be personally involved.

But this woman was different.

She was his half-brother's widow and as such there was a family connection. Her story was heartbreaking.

And yet there was something more. Something that made him want to loosen the grip on her hands and gather her into him and hold.

It was almost a primeval urge. The urge to protect.

The urge to take away her pain any way he knew how.

Which was all getting in the way of what she needed from him, which was to be useful. She was here for a reason. She didn't need him to be messed up with some emotional reaction he didn't understand.

'So what can I do for you, Tasha?' he asked, in a voice he had to force himself to keep steady. 'I'll help in any way I can. Tell me what you need me to do.'

She steadied. He could see her fighting back emotion, turning into the practical woman he sensed she was.

She let go his hands and sat back, and he pushed back too, so the personal link was broken.

'I need an advocate,' she told him. 'No. Emily needs an advocate.'

'Explain.'

She had herself under control again now—sort of.

'I'm only part Australian,' she told him. 'My dad was British but Mum was Australian. I was born here but my parents were in the army. We never had a permanent home. Mum and Dad died when I was fifteen and I went to live with my aunt in the UK. That's where I did medicine. Afterwards I took a job with Médecins Sans Frontières, moving all around the world at need, which is when I met Paul. Paul owned an apartment here so Australia was our base but we still travelled. I've never stayed still long enough to get roots, to make long-term friends. So now I'm in a city I don't know very well. I'm about to deliver Emily by Caesarean section and straight after her birth I'll be expected to make some momentous decisions.'

She faltered then, but forced herself to go on. 'Like…like turning off life support,' she whispered. 'Like accepting what is or isn't possible and not attempting useless heroics. Tom, I don't trust myself but Paul said I could trust you. He spoke of you with affection. You're the only one I could think of.'

And what was he to say to that?

There was only one answer he could give.

'Of course I'll be your advocate,' he told her. 'Or your support person. Tasha, whatever you need, I'll be there for you. You have my word.'

'But you hardly knew Paul.'

'Paul's family and so are you,' he said, and he reached out and took her hands again. 'That's all that matters.'

'Hilda?'

Hilda Brakenworth, Tom's housekeeper, twin of Rhonda, answered the phone with some trepidation. She'd just finished making beef stroganoff and was contemplating the ingredients for a lemon soufflé. 'Make it lovely,' Tom had told her before he'd left for work. 'Alice will be here at eight, just in time for sunset. Can you set the table on the veranda? Candles. Flowers. You know the drill.'

She did, Hilda thought dourly. Tom's idea of a romantic evening never changed. But she was used to his priorities. Medicine came first, surfing second. His love life came a poor third, and the phone call she was receiving now would be like so many she'd received in the past. 'Change of plan,' he'd say and her dinners would go into the freezer or the trash.

'Yes?' she said, mentally consigning her lemon soufflé to oblivion.

'Change of plan. I've invited a guest to stay.'

This was different. 'You want a romantic dinner for three?'

He chuckled but Hilda had known him for a long time. She could hear strain in his voice—strain usually reserved for times when the medical needs of the community were overwhelming.

But did a guest staying warrant stress? She needed to phone Rhonda and find out what was going on.

'I'll put Alice off,' he said. 'She'll understand.'

No, she won't, Hilda decided, thinking of the beautifully groomed, high-maintenance Alice, but she didn't comment.

'Do you want me to make up the front room?'

'I... Yes. And could you put flowers in there?'

'It's a woman?'

'It's a woman called Tasha.' He hesitated and then he told it like it was. 'She's my half-brother's widow and she's in trouble. I'm hoping she'll stay as long as she needs us.'

Cray Point was a tiny, seemingly forgotten backwater, a village on a neck of land stretching out from Port Philip Bay.

'It's one high tide away from being an island, but the medical emergency chopper can get here from Melbourne within half an hour,' Tom told her. 'Your Caesarean's booked in a week and you're not due for two weeks. We're both doctors. We can surely detect early signs of labour and get you to the city fast.'

So a couple of hours after she'd arrived she was on the veranda, trying to eat the beautiful dinner Tom's housekeeper had prepared.

Somewhat to her surprise she did eat. She'd

looked at the meal and felt slightly nauseous, which was pretty much how she'd felt since that appalling last consultation with the cardiologist, but Tom had plonked himself down beside her, scooped stroganoff onto both their plates and directed her attention to the surf.

'It's too flat tonight,' he told her. 'It's been great all day but the wind's died and the waves have died with it. That's the story of my life. I sweat all day trying to finish but the moment my patients stop appearing, so do the good waves. Dawn's better but once I hit the water I forget what I'm booked for. So I have a great time and come in to find Rhonda ready to have my head on a platter and the waiting room bursting at the seams.'

'Rhonda...'

'Rhonda's my receptionist. She and Hilda—she's the housekeeper you just met leaving—are sisters. They rule my life.'

'So no family? No wife and kids?'

'With my family history?' He grinned, a gorgeous, engaging grin that reminded her a little of Paul. 'Paul must have told you about my dad. He did the right thing twice in that he married my mum and then Paul's mother when they were pregnant, but he never stayed around long enough to be a father. He fancied the idea of his sons as his mates but the hard yards were done by our mums, and while they were raising us he went from woman to woman.'

'You think that's genetic?'

He grinned again. 'I reckon it must be. Dating's fun but I'm thirty-four years old and I've never met a woman I'd trust myself to commit to spending the rest of my life with.' His smile faded. 'But, unlike Dad, I won't make promises I can't keep. This life suits me. Mum was born and raised in Cray Point and this community nurtured both of us when Dad walked out on her. I left to do medicine but it's always called me home. The surf's great and the wind here in winter is enough to turn me into a salted kipper. I have a theory that the locals here don't age, they just get more and more preserved. If you dig up the graveyard you'll find old leather.'

'That sounds like you have nothing to do as a doctor.'

'Preserved leather still falls off surfboards,' he said, and the smile came back again. 'And tourists do dumb tourist things. I had a lady yesterday who rented a two-bedroom house for an extended family celebration and wanted it beautifully set up before they arrived. So she blew up eight air beds. On the seventh she started feeling odd but she kept on going. Luckily her landlady dropped in as she keeled over on the eighth. Full infarct. We air ambulanced her to Melbourne and she should make a good recovery but it could have been death by airbed. What a way to go.'

And for the first time in days—weeks?—months?—Tasha found herself chuckling and scooping up the tasty stroganoff. This man may well be a charming womaniser like his father and brother, but at least he was honest about it, she thought. And that side of him didn't affect her. Just for the moment she could put tragedy aside.

As she ate he kept up a stream of small talk, the drama of being a small-town doctor in a town where access could be cut in a moment. As a doctor she found her interest snagged.

'We can't rely on the road,' Tom told her as he attacked some lemon soufflé. 'It floods. It also takes one minor traffic accident or one broken-down car to prevent access for hours or even days. As a village we're pretty self-reliant and the medical helicopter evac team is brilliant. You sure you don't want more of this?'

'I... No.' She'd surprised herself by eating any at all.

'We'll feed you up for the next week,' Tom said calmly. 'You and Emily. Did you know there are studies that say taste comes through? This is a truly excellent lemon soufflé. Who's to say that Emily isn't enjoying it, too?'

It was an odd thought. Unconsciously her hands went to her belly, and Tom's voice softened.

'Cuddling's good,' he told her. 'I bet she can feel that as well, and I know she can hear us talking.'

'She might...' Her voice cracked. 'But the doctor said...'

'I know what's been said,' Tom told her, and his hand reached over and held hers, strong and firm—a wash of stability in a world that had tilted so far she'd felt she must surely fall. 'But, Tasha, your baby's alive now. She's being cuddled. She's sharing your lemon soufflé and she's listening to the surf. That's not such a bad life for a baby.'

It was a weird concept. That Emily could feel her now...

And suddenly Emily kicked, a good solid kick that even Tom could see under her bulky windcheater. They both looked at the bulge as Emily changed position, and something inside her settled. The appalling maelstrom of emotions took a back seat.

She was here overlooking the sea, feeding her baby lemon soufflé. It was true, Emily could hear the surf—every book said that babies could hear.

'Maybe you could take her for a swim tomorrow,' Tom suggested. 'Lie in the shallows and let the water wash over you—and her. She'll feel your body rocking and she'll hear the water whooshing around. How cool would that be, young Emily?'

And he got it.

She looked up at him in stupefaction but Tom was gazing out to sea again, as if he'd said nothing of importance.

But he'd said it.

How cool would that be, young Emily?

No matter how short Emily's life would be, for now, for this moment, Emily was real. She was her own little person, and with that simple statement Tom was acknowledging it.

The tangle of grief and fear and anger fell away. It was there for the future—she knew that—but for now she was eating lemon soufflé and tomorrow was for tomorrow. For now Emily was alive and kicking. She had no need for her faulty heart. She was safe.

And for the moment Tasha felt safe, too. When Tom had suggested staying she'd thought she'd agree to one night, when she could get to know him so she could figure whether she really could trust him to be her advocate. She knew if the birth was difficult and there were hard decisions to be made then she'd need a friend.

And suddenly she had one.

Thank you, Paul, she thought silently, and it was one of the very few times when she'd thought of Paul with gratitude. He had pretty much been the kid who never grew up, a Peter Pan, a guy who looked on the world as an amazing adventure. His love of life had drawn her in but she hadn't been married for long before she'd realised that life for Paul was one amazing adventure after another. Putting his life at risk—and hers too if the need arose—was his drug of choice.

And as for Tom saying his father's womanising was a genetic fault…yeah, Paul had pretty much proved that.

But now… He'd died but he'd left his sperm and it seemed he'd also left her a link to a man who could help her. Tom might be a womaniser like his brother. He might be any number of things, but right now he was saying exactly what she needed to hear. And then he was falling silent, letting the night, the warmth, the gentle murmur of the sea do his talking for him.

She could trust him for now, she thought, and once more her hands tightened on her belly.

She could trust this man to be her baby's advocate.

And her friend?

By the time dinner ended Tasha looked almost asleep. Tom had shown her to his best spare room and she hit the pillow as if she hadn't slept for a month. As maybe she hadn't.

Tom checked on her fifteen minutes after he'd shown her to her bedroom. He knocked lightly and then opened the door a sliver. He'd thought if she was lying awake, staring at the ceiling, he could organise music or maybe a talking book.

She was deeply asleep. Her soft brown curls were splayed out over the pillows and one of her hands was out from under the sheets, stretched as if in supplication.

She hadn't closed the curtains. In the moonlight her look of appalling fatigue had faded.

She looked at peace.

He stood and looked at her for a long moment, fighting a stupid but almost irresistible urge to stoop over the bed and hold her. Protect her.

It was because she was family, he told himself, but he knew it wasn't.

Impending tragedy? Not that either, he thought. In his years as a country doctor he'd pretty much seen it all. Experience didn't make him immune. When this community hurt, he hurt, but he could handle it.

He wasn't sure he could handle this woman's hurt.

And it wasn't being helpful, staring down at her in the moonlight. It might even be construed as creepy. Like father, like son? He gave himself a fast mental shake, backed out and closed the door.

He headed to his study. Tasha had handed her medical file to him diffidently back at the surgery. 'If you're going to be our advocate you need to know the facts.'

So he hit the internet, searching firstly for the combination of the problems in Emily's heart and then on the background of the paediatric cardiologist who had her in his charge.

The information made him feel ill. He was trawling the internet for hope, and he couldn't find it.

He rang a friend of a friend, a cardiologist in the States. He rang another in London.

There was no joy from either.

In the end he headed back out to the veranda. This was a great old house, slightly ramshackle, built of ancient timber with a corrugated-iron roof and a veranda that ran all the way around. It was settled back from the dunes, overlooking the sea. The house had belonged to his grandparents and then his mother. It was a place of peace but it wasn't giving him peace now.

This child was what...his half-niece? He'd scarcely known Paul and he'd only just met Tasha. Why should this prognosis be so gut-wrenching?

He couldn't afford to get emotional, he told himself. Tasha needed him to be clear-headed, an advocate, someone who could stand back and see the situation dispassionately.

Maybe she should find someone else.

There wasn't anyone else—or maybe there was,

but suddenly he knew that even if there was he wouldn't relinquish the role.

He wanted to be by her side.

Her image flooded back, the pale face on the pillow, the hand stretched out...

It was doing his head in.

It was three in the morning and he had house calls scheduled before morning's clinic.

'That's the first thing to organise,' he said out loud, trying to find peace in practicality. At least that was easy. Mary and Chris were a husband-and-wife team, two elderly doctors who'd moved to Cray Point in semi-retirement. They'd helped out in an emergency before and he knew they would now.

'Because this is family,' he said out loud, and the thought was strange.

The woman sleeping in his guest room, the woman who looked past the point of exhaustion, the woman who was twisting his heart in a way he didn't understand...was family?

CHAPTER TWO

Eighteen months later...

THE SURF WAS EXTRAORDINARY. It was also dangerous. The wind had changed ten minutes ago, making the sea choppy and unpredictable.

The morning's swells had enticed every surfer in the district to brave the winter's chill, but a sudden wind change had caught them by surprise. The wind was now catching the waves as the swell rolled out again, with force that had wave smashing against wave.

Most surfers had opted for safety and headed for shore, but not Tom. There were three teenagers who hadn't given up yet, three kids he knew well. Alex, James and Rowan were always egging themselves on, pushing past the limits of sensible.

As the wind had changed he'd headed over to them. 'Time to get out, boys,' he'd told them. 'This surf's pushing into the reef.'

'This is just getting exciting,' Alex had jeered. 'You go home, old man. Leave the good stuff for us.'

They were idiots, but they were kids and he was worried. He'd backed off, staying behind the breakers while he waited for them to see sense.

Maybe he was getting old.

He was thirty-six, which wasn't so old in the scheme of things. Susie was coming to dinner tonight and Susie was gorgeous. She was thirty-seven, a divorcee with a couple of kids, but she looked and acted a whole lot younger.

If she was here she'd be pushing him to ride the waves, he thought, instead of sitting out here like a wuss.

He glanced at the kids, who were still hoping for a clean wave. Idiots.

Was it safe to leave them? He still had to walk up to the headland before dinner, to take this week's photograph for Tasha.

And that set him thinking. He'd promised the photographs but were they still needed? Was anything still needed? She didn't say. He tried to write emails that would connect as a friend, but her responses were curt to the point of non-existent.

Maybe he reminded her of a pain that was almost overwhelming.

Maybe he was doing it for himself.

For Tom had stayed at Tasha's side for all of Emily's short life and it still seemed natural to keep tending her grave. In the few short days he'd helped care for the baby girl, she'd twisted her way around his heart.

But if Emily's death still hurt him, how was Tasha doing? She never said.

Suddenly, lying out behind the breakers, overseeing idiots taking risks, he had a ridiculous urge to take the next plane and find out.

Which was crazy. He was Tasha's link to her baby, nothing more, and she probably no longer wanted that.

But then he needed to stop thinking of Tasha.

A massive swell was building behind him, and the wind was swirling. He glanced towards the shore and saw the wave that had just broken was surging back from the beach. It was almost at a right angle to the wave coming in.

But the teenagers weren't looking at the beach. They were staring over their shoulders, waiting for the incoming wave.

'No!' He yelled with all the power he could muster. 'It'll take you onto the reef. No!'

The two boys nearest heard. Alex and James. They faltered and let the wave power under them.

But Rowan either hadn't heard or hadn't wanted to hear. He caught the wave with ease and let its power sweep him forward.

It was too late to yell again, for the outgoing wave was heading inexorably for them all. For Tom and Alex and James it was simply a matter of head down, hold fast, ride through it. For Rowan, though... He was upright on the board when the walls of water smashed together.

The reef was too close. Rowan was under water, caught by his ankle rope, dragged by the sheer force of the waves.

He was on the reef.

Tom put his head down and headed straight for him.

There was no email.

Every Sunday since she'd returned to England Tom had sent an email, and there wasn't one now.

At first she wasn't bothered. Tom was a lone medical practitioner. Things happened. He'd send it later.

He didn't…and so she went to bed feeling empty.

Which was stupid.

It had been eighteen months since Emily's death. She'd left Australia as soon as the formalities were over, desperate to put the pain behind her. She hadn't had the energy to head back to her work with Médicins Sans Frontières. Instead she'd taken a job in an emergency department in London and tried to drown herself in her job.

Mostly it was okay. Mostly she got to the end of the day thinking she could face the next.

And Tom's emails helped. He sent one every Sunday, short messages with a little local gossip, snippets of his life, his latest love interest, any interesting cases he'd treated. And at the end he always attached a photograph of Emily's grave.

Sometimes the grave was rain-washed, sometimes it was bathed in sunshine, but it was always covered in wildflowers and backed by the sea. He'd promised this on the day of the funeral and he'd kept his word. 'I'll look after this for you, Tasha. I'll look after it for Emily and I'll always make sure you can see it.'

It hurt but still she wanted it. She usually sent

a curt thank you back and felt guilty that she couldn't do better.

For Tom had been wonderful, she conceded. He'd been with her every step of the way during that appalling time.

It had been Tom who'd intervened when various specialists had decreed Emily needed to be in ICU, saying that spending time with her mother would decrease her tiny life span. Tom had simply looked at them and they'd backed off.

It had been Tom who'd organised discreet, empathic photographers, who'd put together her most treasured possession—an album of a perfect, beautiful baby being held with love.

It had been Tom who'd taken her back to Cray Point, who'd stood beside her during a heartbreaking burial and then let her be, to sit on the veranda and stare out at the horizon for as long as she'd needed. He'd been there when she'd felt like talking and had left her alone when she'd needed to be alone.

And when, three weeks after Emily's death, she'd woken one morning and said she needed to go back to London, she needed to go back to work, he'd driven her to the airport and he'd hugged her goodbye.

She'd felt as if leaving him had been ripping yet another part of her life away.

But his emails had come every Sunday, and he was seemingly not bothered that she could hardly respond.

'So what?' she demanded of herself when there was still no email the next morning. 'Tom was there when you needed him but it's been eighteen months. You can't expect him to photograph a grave for the rest of his life.'

Could she move on, too?

And with that came another thought. The idea had seeped into her consciousness a couple of months ago. It was stupid. She surely wasn't brave enough to do it, but once it had seeded in her brain the longing it brought with it wouldn't let her alone.

Could she try for another baby?

What would Tom think? she wondered, and her instinctive question was enough to make her stop walking and blink.

'Tom's not in the equation,' she said out loud, and the people around her cast her curious glances.

She shook her head and kept going. Of course Tom wasn't in the equation.

'It's good that the contact's finally over,' she told herself, but then she thought of Emily's grave at Cray Point and knew that part of her heart would always be there.

With or without Tom Blake.

CHAPTER THREE

Six weeks later...

TODAY HAD BEEN an exhausting shift in the emergency department of her London hospital. The hospital was on the fringe of a poor socio-economic district, where unemployment was rife and where the young didn't have enough to do. The combination was a recipe for disaster and the disasters often ended up in Tasha's care.

She'd had two stabbings this shift. She was emotionally wiped—but, then, she thought as she changed to go home, she wanted to be emotionally wiped. She wanted to go home exhausted enough to sleep.

She'd hardly slept for weeks. Why?

Was it because the emails had stopped?

It was her own fault, she thought. She hadn't made it clear she was grateful, because a part of her wasn't. Tom's emails were a jagged reminder of past pain. She didn't want to remember—but neither did she want to forget.

And now Tom had obviously decided it was time to move on. She should be over it.

Could she ever be *over it*? She stared at her reflection in the change-room mirror and let her thoughts take her where they willed. How to move on?

Part of her ached for another baby, but did she have the courage?

'Tasha? You have visitors.' Ellen, the nurse administrator, put her nose around the door. 'Two ladies are here to see you. They arrived two hours ago. They wouldn't let me disturb you but said as soon as you finished your shift could I let you know. I've popped them into the counselling room with tea and biccies. They seem nice.'

'Nice?'

Emergency departments saw many tragedies. Often family members came in, days, weeks, sometimes months after the event to talk through what had happened. Ellen usually pre-empted contact by finding the patient file and giving her time to read it. It helped. For doctors like Tasha, after weeks or months individual deaths could become blurred.

But Ellen wasn't carrying a file and she'd described them as nice, nothing more.

'It's personal,' Ellen said, seeing her confusion. 'They say it's nothing to do with a patient. They're Australian. Hilda and Rhonda. Middle-aged. One's knitting, the other's doing crochet.'

Hilda and Rhonda.

She stilled, thinking of the only two Australians she knew who were called Hilda and Rhonda.

'Shall I tell them you can't see them?' Ellen asked, watching her face. 'I'm sure they'll understand. They seem almost nervous about disturbing you. One word from me and I suspect they'll scuttle.'

Did she want them to...scuttle?

No. Of course she didn't.

For some reason her heart was doing some sort of stupid lurch. Surely something wasn't wrong? With Tom?

It couldn't be, she thought. He'd be safe home in Cray Point with his latest lady. Who? He'd mentioned his women in his emails. Alice? No, Alice had been a good twelve months ago. There'd been Kylie and Samantha and Susie since then.

The Blake brothers were incorrigible, she thought, and she even managed a sort of smile as she headed off to see what Rhonda and Hilda had in store for her.

But they weren't here to tell her about Tom's latest lady.

'A subarachnoid haemorrhage?' She stared at the two women in front of her and she couldn't believe what she was hearing. 'Tom's had a subarachnoid haemorrhage?'

The women had greeted her with disbelief at first—'You look so different!'

'I'm wearing scrubs,' she'd told them, but they'd shaken their heads in unison.

'You look prettier. Younger. Though that time would have made anyone look old.' They'd hugged her, but then they'd moved onto Tom.

These two women had formed a caring background during her time in Cray Point but now they seemed almost apologetic. Apologising for what they were telling her.

'It was the surf,' Rhonda said. 'A minor accident, he said, just a cut needing a few stitches, but then his neck was stiff and he got a blinding headache. He collapsed, scaring the life out of us. We had to get the air ambulance and the doctors say he only just made it.'

'But they say he's going to be okay,' Hilda broke in, speaking fast. Maybe she'd seen the colour drain from Tasha's face. 'Eventually. But it did some damage—the same as a minor stroke. Now he's trying to pretend it's business as normal but of course it's not.'

'What happened?' Tasha asked, stunned.

'It was the first of the winter storms,' Hilda told her, sniffing at the idiocy of surfers in general and one surfer in particular. 'The surf was huge and of course people were doing stupid things. They were surfing too close to the rocks for the conditions and he hit his head—a nasty, deep gash. Mary and Chris...did you meet them? They're the medical couple who help out sometimes. They stitched his head and tried to persuade him he needed a scan but would he listen? And that night... Well, it was lucky I decided to stay on, though cleaning the pantry was an excuse. He'd put off having his latest woman for dinner so I thought he must be feeling really ill. And he was toying with his meal when all of a sudden he said "Hilda, my neck... My head..." And then he sort of slumped.'

'There was no loss of consciousness but by the time the ambulance arrived he couldn't move his left arm or leg,' Rhonda told her. She took a deep breath and recited something she must have learned off by heart. 'His scans showed a skull fracture and infarct in the right lentiform nucleus corona radiata.'

'That's in the brain,' Hilda said helpfully, and Rhonda rolled her eyes. But then she got serious again.

'Anyway, the air ambulance was there fast and got him to Melbourne. They operated within the hour and they're saying long-term he should be fine. He spent two weeks in hospital, protesting every minute. Then they wanted him to go to rehab but he wouldn't. He says he can do the exercises himself. So now he's back in Cray Point, pretending it's business as usual.'

'But it's not,' Hilda told her. 'He has left-sided weakness. He's not allowed to drive. The doctors only let him come home on the condition he has physio every day but of course he says he's too busy to do it. He should concentrate on rehab for at least two months but will he?'

'He doesn't have time,' Hilda told her. 'And I was dusting in his study and he'd requested a copy of the specialist's letters and I just...happened to read them. Anyway the specialist's saying there's a risk of permanent residual damage if he doesn't follow orders. But Mary and Chris have a new grandbaby in Queensland, their daughter's ill and they had to go. There's no other doctor to help.'

'And of course it's winter in Australia.' Rhonda took over seamlessly. 'No doctor will take on a locum job in Cray Point in winter. We know he advertised—we weren't supposed to know that either but...'

'Hilda saw it on his study desk?' Tasha suggested, and Hilda flushed and then smiled.

'Well, I did, dear. But of course no one answered, and the oldies in Cray Point are still getting ill and he knows how much they need him. He cares too much to let us look after ourselves. So he's hobbling around, still working. The night before we left there was a car crash and out he went. It was filthy weather and he was crawling into the wreckage to stop bleeding...'

'And then we had to leave.' Up until now Rhonda had sounded resigned, full of the foolishness of men, but suddenly her voice wobbled. 'You know we're both English? We married brothers and moved to Cray Point thirty years ago but our parents stayed here. Last week our mam died and our dad's in a mess so we had to drop everything and come. Including abandoning Tom. We'll take our dad home with us but first there's his house to be sorted, immigration, so much to do...'

'But we're worrying about Tom all the time,' Hilda told her. 'We know he's not coping. It'll be weeks before we can get back, and who's to boss him around? He'll push himself and push himself. We have one district nurse and no one else. Cray Point's in real trouble. And then in the middle of last night Rhonda sat up in bed and said, "What about Tasha? She's family."'

The word seemed to echo around the counselling room.

Family.

'I knew nothing about this,' she said faintly, and Rhonda nodded.

'Well, of course you wouldn't. He doesn't talk to anyone about it, and of course he worries about you. We all do. He'd never bother you. Tasha... dear, it seems really unfair to ask, but Hilda knew your address...'

'From Tom's desk?' She couldn't help herself but she won a couple of half-hearted smiles.

'Well, yes, dear,' Hilda agreed. 'Though of

course I didn't go looking. I just happened to have seen it on a certificate he left out for me to post to you. So we knew you were living in a hospital apartment and I remembered which hospital. So we thought we'd just come and let you know...'

'Because he needs someone,' Rhonda told her. And then she paused and told it like it was. 'He needs you.'

To say Tasha's mind was in overdrive was an understatement. She'd just finished a frantic shift. Normally it took hours to debrief herself, to rid herself of the images of the various crises bursting through the ambulance doors, but suddenly all she could think of was Tom.

The sudden end to contact hadn't been because he thought she should move on. It had been because he was in trouble himself.

'W-what about Susie?' she stammered. The thought of Tom needing her was such a switch that it had her unbalanced. 'Can't she help?'

And the two women snorted in unison.

'One thing Dr Tom Blake can't do and that's choose a woman who's any use,' Rhonda declared. 'She's hardly been near him since his accident. And she's not a doctor or even a nurse.

How can she help? You're a doctor, dear. That's why we're here.'

'You want me to go?' Even saying it sounded wrong.

But both women were trying to smile. Their smiles were nervous. Their smiles said they didn't hold out much hope but they were like headlights, catching her and holding her. She couldn't move.

'Could you?' Hilda sounded breathless.

'Is it possible?' Rhonda whispered.

She stood and stared at the two rotund little ladies. They stared back, their eyes full of hope. And doubt. And just a touch of guilt as well.

Tom...

He needed her.

She didn't want to go.

Why not?

She could go. She knew she could. There'd been an intake of brand-new doctors only last week and there was crossover from the last lot. Her shift could be covered.

She could walk out of her barren little apartment within an hour.

But to go to Tom...

She didn't want to go back to Australia. Australia was full of memories of her little girl, her little fighter who'd lived just seven days. How could she go back to the place of all that pain?

But there was more to this than grief, she acknowledged. Her reaction wasn't all about not wanting to be where Emily had lived and died, and she had the courage to acknowledge it. She'd never avoided thinking about Emily and, to be fair, Tom had had a hand in that. He'd been with her all that time.

It was Tom who'd made sure she'd shared every precious moment of Emily's tiny life. It was Tom who'd sat by her, fielding well-meaning professionals, admitting those who could help, firmly turning away those who couldn't.

There had been so much support. There had been so much love.

For Tom had loved, too. 'She's my niece,' he'd told her when she'd been so exhausted she'd had to sleep but the thought of closing her eyes on her little girl had been unbearable. 'You sleep and I'll hold her every single moment. And I promise I won't sleep while you've entrusted her to me.'

He'd just...been there. She could hardly think of Emily without thinking of Tom.

And then, after Emily had died...

Being bundled back to Cray Point. A simple,

beautiful ceremony on the headland because she couldn't think where else was right. Then sleeping and sleeping and sleeping, while Tom picked up the threads of...being Tom.

Which included his women. Alice was there, vaguely resentful of Tasha's presence. And then Alice was no longer around and Tasha knew it was partly because of her.

She'd said something to him—apologised—and Tom had grinned. 'Don't fuss yourself, lassie,' he'd told her. 'Alice knows I don't take my love life seriously. The whole town knows it.'

So he was like Paul. That was the thought that was holding her rigid now.

He was lovely, kind, gentle, caring.

He went from woman to woman.

He'd just suffered a cerebral bleed from a surfing accident. He was yet another man who took crazy risks...

The Blake brothers spelled trouble. She didn't want to go anywhere near him, but she owed him so much.

She thought of him now, the image that was burned into her mind. Waking up from sleep and finding him crooning down to her little daughter.

'Surfing's awesome,' he'd been telling her tiny

baby. 'The feel of cool water on your toes, the strength of the wave lifting you, surging forward... Feel my fingers as I push under your toes. Imagine that's a wave, lifting you, surging... That's right, our Emily, curl your toes. You have such a tiny life, our Emily, but we need to fill it with so much. I wish I could take you surfing but feel the power under your toes and know that surfing's wonderful and you're wonderful and I hope you can take all this with you.'

And Tasha found herself blinking and Hilda gasped and glared at Rhonda, who grabbed a handful of tissues from the counselling table. Tasha suddenly found she was being hugged. 'Dear, no,' Rhonda gasped. 'We shouldn't have come. We never should have asked. Tom will be okay. Cray Point will survive. Forget it, sweetheart, forget we ever came.'

Somehow she disengaged from their collective hug. Somewhere she'd read a research article that said hugging released oxytocin and oxytocin did all sorts of good things to the body. It made you more empathic. It made you want to connect more with your fellow humans.

With Tom? She'd be playing with fire.

Why? Because he was like Paul? He wasn't.

Not really. She'd stayed with him for a month and there'd never been a hint that he was interested in her...that way.

Besides, she was older, wiser, and she knew how to protect herself.

And this time she didn't need Tom. Tom needed her, and Rhonda and Hilda were waiting for an answer.

And in the end there was only one answer she could give. No matter what Tom's personal life was like, what he'd done for her had been beyond price.

And then the idea that had been playing at the edges of her mind suddenly, unexpectedly surfaced. The idea had been growing, like an insistent ache, an emptiness demanding to be filled, a void it took courage to even think about.

She could still scarcely think about it but if she went to help Tom she'd be returning to Australia, where an IVF clinic still held Paul's gift.

She'd agonised over using Paul's sperm last time, but in the end it had come down to thinking her baby could know of its father. This time the tug to use the same sperm was stronger. Another baby would be Emily's brother or sister.

And suddenly that was in her heart, front and centre, and she knew what her answer would be.

'Of course I'll go,' she told them swiftly, before she had the time to change her mind. Before fear took over. 'It'll take me a couple of days to get there but I'll do it.'

'Oh, Tasha,' Hilda breathed.

'But don't tell him,' Rhonda urged. 'He won't let you come if you tell him. He'll say he's fine. He'll fire us for contacting you.'

'I'd like to see him try,' Hilda declared, but she sounded nervous and Tasha summoned a grin.

'Okay,' she told them. 'I won't warn him. But he'd better not be in bed with Susie when I get there.'

'I wouldn't think so,' Hilda declared, though she didn't sound absolutely certain.

'Sure,' Tasha said, but she didn't feel sure in the least.

CHAPTER FOUR

THERE WERE THINGS to do and he should be doing them. It was driving him nuts.

Old Mrs Carstairs hadn't had a house call for weeks. She'd been hospitalised with pneumonia in late autumn and it had left her weak. She should be staying with her daughter in Melbourne but she'd refused to stay away from her house a moment longer.

And who could blame her? Tom thought morosely. Margaret Carstairs owned a house high on the headland overlooking the sweeping vista of Bass Strait. She was content to lie on her day bed and watch the changing weather, the sea, and the whales making their great migration north. She was content to let the world come to her.

Except the world couldn't. Or Tom couldn't. And unlike Margaret Carstairs, he was far from happy to lie on a couch and watch the sea. Any reports about Margaret came from the district nurse and he knew Brenda was worried.

But he couldn't drive and he'd have trouble walking down Margaret's steep driveway when he got there. When he'd first woken after surgery he'd been almost completely paralysed down his left side. His recovery had been swift, but not swift enough. He still had a dragging weakness, and terror had been replaced by frustration.

He couldn't ignore his body's weakness. He couldn't drive. He used Karen, the local taxi driver, but since his leg had let him down while crawling into a crashed car, even Karen was imposing limits.

'He would have died if I hadn't done it,' he muttered to no one in particular. It was true. The driver had perforated a lung. It had been a complex procedure to get him out alive and if Tom had waited for paramedics it would have been too late. The fact that he'd become trapped himself when his leg hadn't had the strength to push himself out was surely minor. It was an excellent result.

But he still couldn't drive and he still had trouble walking in this hilly, clifftop town. So here he was, waiting for the next emergency that he couldn't go to.

His phone went and he lunged for it, willing it to be something he could handle.

It wasn't.

Old Bill Hadley lived down the steepest steps in Cray Point. He was lying at the bottom of them now, whimpering into his cellphone.

'Doc? I know you're crook, but I reckon I might have sprained me ankle. I'm stuck at the bottom of the steps. I've yelled but no one can hear me. Middle of the day, everyone must be out. Lucky I had me phone, don't you think? Do you reckon you could come?'

Bill Hadley was tough. If he was saying he might have sprained his ankle it was probably a fracture. Tom could hear the pain in the old man's voice, but he couldn't go. Not down those steps.

'I'll call the ambulance and get the district nurse to come and stay with you until it arrives,' he told Bill, and he heard silence and he knew there was pain involved. A lot of pain. 'Brenda can stabilise your ankle and keep you comfortable.'

'She…she can give me an injection, like?'

'She can.' Once again he felt that sweep of helplessness. He could authorise drugs over the phone but it was a risk. Bill had pre-existing conditions. Without being able to assess the whole situation...

He couldn't.

'Sorry, Bill, it's the best I can do,' he told him. 'Just keep that ankle still. There's no other way.'

And then he was interrupted. 'Yes, there is.'

He looked up from the settee and he almost dropped the phone.

Tasha was standing in the doorway.

Tasha...

This was a Tasha he'd never seen before. Tasha on the other side of tragedy?

When last he'd seen her she'd been post-pregnancy and ravaged by grief. Her hair had needed a cut. She'd abandoned wearing make-up and she'd worn nothing but baggy jogging pants and windcheaters. Even the day he'd put her on the plane to return to England he'd thought she'd looked like she'd just emerged from a war zone.

This woman, though, was wearing neat black pants and a crisp white shirt, tucked in to accentuate a slender waist. A pale blue sweater was looped around her shoulders. Her curls were shiny and bouncing, let loose to wisp around her shoulders.

She looked cool, elegant...beautiful.

She was carrying a suitcase. She set it down and smiled, and her smile was bright and professional.

'Hi,' she said, and beamed.

'H-hi.' Her smile almost knocked him into the middle of next week, but she was already switching to professional.

'Are you knocking back work? When I've come all this way to do as much work as possible? An injured ankle? Bill who?'

'Bill Hadley...'

'Ankle injury? House call? That's what I'm here for.'

'What the—?'

'Is it urgent? Is it okay if I use your car? Or I can ring the taxi again. I'll need his patient file if there is one, and an address. Can I use your medical kit?'

Tom couldn't answer. It felt like all the oxygen had been sucked out of the room. All the oxygen was in her smile.

She shook her head in mock exasperation and lifted the phone from his grasp.

'Bill? I've come in on the end of this conversation but this is Tasha Raymond. I'm Dr Blake's sister-in-law, a doctor, too, and I'm here to help until Tom's on his feet again. Could you tell me what the problem is?'

'You can drive?' Tom could hear Bill's quavering hope.

'I can,' Tasha assured him. 'You'll have heard that Dr Blake's had an accident, so we need to look after him. That means using me until he's recovered. What's happened?'

There was a moment's pause and then, 'I reckon I've sprained me ankle. If you could come, Doc, that'd be great.'

Doc. The transition was seamless, Tom thought, astounded. The community was desperate for a doctor and Tasha was here. Therefore Tasha was *Doc.*

'Five minutes tops,' Tasha said, as Bill explained the problem and outlined where he lived. 'I walked down those very steps when I was here eighteen months ago. Hang in there.'

And she disconnected and turned to Tom. 'Hey,' she said, and gave him her very warmest smile. 'It's good to see you. I'm so sorry about your accident but Rhonda and Hilda say you need me and it seems they're right. We can talk later but this sounds like I should go. Patient history? Anything else I should know?'

'You can't.' He was feeling like he'd been punched in the solar plexus. This was a whirlwind and it wasn't stopping. 'Tasha, I'm coping. I'll go.'

And her smile softened to one of understanding. And sympathy. 'How weak is your leg, scale one to ten?' she said gently. 'Ten's strong. One's useless.'

'Eight,' he said, and she fixed him with a don't-mess-with-the-doctor look.

'Really?'

'Okay, six,' he conceded. 'But—'

'I didn't fly from London for buts. I flew from London because you've been injured, you need care and Cray Point needs me.' She stooped then and brushed her lips against his forehead, a faint touch. A sisterly gesture? 'I'm so sorry you've been hurt but for now it seems you need to rest. Can I take your car?'

He stared and she gazed calmly back. Waiting for him to accept the inevitable.

He had no choice. She'd flown all the way from England to help him. He should be grateful.

He was grateful but he was also...overwhelmed? That she come all this way...

Tasha was the one who needed help, not him, but for now...he had no choice.

'I'd appreciate your help,' he said stiffly. 'I... Thank you. But, Tasha, I'm coming with you.'

She drove. He sat in the passenger seat and tried to get his head around what had just happened.

A whirlwind had arrived. A woman he scarcely recognised.

The last time he'd seen Tasha she'd been limp with shock and grief. Now she was a woman in charge of her world. She was doctor reacting to a medical call with professional efficiency.

She was a woman who looked, quite simply, gorgeous.

His head wasn't coping.

He directed while she drove but she would have gotten there fine without him. In the weeks after Emily's death she'd walked Cray Point, over and over. He'd thought she'd hardly seen it. She obviously had.

'So...Rhonda and Hilda...' he said at last. It was almost the first question he'd been able to ask. She'd been all brisk efficiency, checking his medical supplies, watching him—as if she wasn't sure could manage—climb into the car, then turning towards Bill's like a homing pigeon. It was as if she'd been a doctor here for years.

'They came to see me in London,' she was saying. 'They told me you were in trouble.'

'They had no right.'

'They had every right.' Her voice softened. 'Eighteen months ago Cray Point was here when I needed it. So were you, but if we're taking the personal out of it then I'm paying back Cray Point.'

'So you just dropped everything…'

'As you dropped everything for me. I didn't leave anyone in the lurch, as you didn't. Next question?'

He sat back and tried to think of questions. He had a thousand.

He couldn't think of any.

And she had the temerity to grin. 'Very good, Dr Blake.'

'You want to say "Good boy" and pat my head?'

Her smile widened. 'Not yet. You have two months of behaving yourself before you get any elephant stamps.'

'Behaving myself?'

'Doing what the doctor says. Lots of rest. Lots of rehabilitation. Rhonda says you should be going to physio daily, but you won't leave Cray Point with no doctor. She also says you hurt more than you let on, and that you're not sleeping.'

'How does she know?'

She chuckled. 'Their intelligence system is awesome. I'm to report back.'

'Maybe you should stay somewhere else,' he said, but her smile didn't slip.

'Maybe I should, and I can, if you want privacy. All I care about is that you can get to rehab. What you do is your business as long as you're tucked up in bed when your doctor says you should be.' She considered for a moment and then added. 'Probably by yourself? I'm willing to bet that nights of endless passion aren't what your doctors are ordering.'

They weren't. He stared down at his weak leg with loathing.

'Nights of passion aren't exactly on the agenda,' he said through gritted teeth, and she chuckled again.

'I'll give you your elephant stamp for that one. It's this street, isn't it?'

Cray Point was an historic fishing village perched on a high headland. A few of the older houses were built at the foot of the cliffs, with narrow flights of steps twisting down to their entrances. They were a nightmare to access, increasingly owned and maintained by holiday-makers who didn't mind a few weeks of carting groceries down a hundred steps. Bill was one of the last fishermen living in one.

'History?' she demanded as they pulled to a halt, and somehow Tom pulled himself together and told her that Bill was an unstable diabetic.

'He's put on a power of weight since he stopped fishing, though heaven knows how he manages it when he has to come up and down these steps. He's had diabetes for years but he lives on fish and chips and beer, and takes his insulin when he feels like it. He's had more than one hypo. I suspect one might have contributed to this fall. He has peripheral nerve damage to his feet.'

'Yikes,' Tasha said. 'Okay, you stay up here and direct the ambulance.'

'Do I have a choice?'

She grinned again, an endearing grin that if he wasn't so frustrated he might even enjoy. 'No,' she told him. 'But you may be useful. I'll ring for advice if I need it.'

'Why does that sound so patronising?'

'Because Rhonda and Hilda say you need patronising,' she told him, and before he could begin to realise what she intended she leaned across and kissed him. It was a feather kiss, the merest brush of lips against his nose. Why it had the power to pack a jolt as fierce as an electric charge...

But she was out of the car and in the back seat, fetching his doctor's bag, before he had a chance to analyse it.

'See you later,' she told him. 'Be good.'

He was left in the car to glower.

Bill had fractured his ankle. She suspected he also had fractured ribs. His blood sugar was so low it was a wonder he wasn't unconscious and it took skill to get him stabilised.

If she hadn't been here the outcome might have been fatal, she thought as she worked, and as Brenda, the district nurse, came bustling down the steps and immediately starting to berate Bill for living in such a dumb place, she was sure of it.

'Leave him be,' she said gently. She'd packed him with insulating sheets to keep him warm. She had a drip up and drugs on board and she'd given him enough glucose to get his sugars up but he was drifting in and out of consciousness regardless.

'And Doc shouldn't be out,' Brenda scolded. 'There he is, sitting at the top of the steps, and it's cold. You should make him stay home.'

That warranted an inward smile. She'd been in Cray Point for an hour and already she was being treated as part of the furniture. That's what it was like to be needed, she thought. There'd been a gap here and she'd slipped seamlessly into it.

'Tasha?' It was Tom.

She'd conceded his need to know and had left her phone on speaker. Tom might be up the top of the cliff, but in spirit—and in voice—he was right there.

'Yep?' She was adjusting the drip, wondering whether it was worth trying to move him inside.

'The ambulance is five minutes away,' Tom told her, and she relaxed a little. Bill's breathing was starting to get shallow. Shock, or something more sinister?

'Excellent.'

'You're worried.' He'd got it, she thought. Her one word must have contained a thread of concern.

'Nothing we can't handle,' she said brightly.

Bill was looking up at her, dazed. The last thing she wanted was to frighten him.

'He looks like death, Dr Blake,' Brenda breathed. 'He looks awful.'

And Tasha gave her a glare that would have curdled milk.

'He does.' How to turn this around? 'He looks like he hasn't washed for days and he smells like dead fish,' she told Tom. 'Bill, I don't know what you've been doing but I suspect the first thing the nurses do in their nice clean hospital is give you a wash. Nurses are fussy about who they put between their sheets.'

Amazingly Bill managed a faint chuckle and Tasha chuckled, too, and then they settled back to wait for the ambulance.

She was stunning.

He sat in the car and directed the paramedics down the steps when they arrived and he felt the weight of the world lift from his shoulders.

She'd come from half a world away to help him.

He wanted to be down those steps instead of her, he thought, and then he thought, no, he wanted to be down there *with* her.

Tasha.

He'd thought of her almost every day since she'd left. He'd thought of tapering off the dumb, newsy emails he'd sent her but sending a photograph of a grave without a note seemed wrong, and somehow the contact seemed important. He was family and he had to show he cared.

And here she was. Family. Caring.

The thought did his head in. He was the carer and yet she'd abandoned her life and come to help him.

The paramedics brought Bill up the steps strapped onto a stretcher and Tom eased himself out of the car to greet him. To his amazement, Bill was recovering his good humour.

'Practically don't hurt at all now, Doc,' he told him. 'Tasha fixed me right up. She's a good 'un and she says she's staying till you're better. Cray Point's lucky. You're lucky.'

Behind him, Brenda was talking to Tasha, and he realised his nurse was outlining home-care visits for the next day.

'Hey,' he said, interrupting Brenda's riveting account of Doris Mayberry's leg abscess. 'I haven't employed Tasha yet.'

And Brenda looked astonished. 'What do you mean, you haven't employed her? She's here to work and we need her. What possible quibble could you have?'

Quibble? He tried to think of any.

'Do you have registration to work in Australia?' he asked.

'Of course,' Tasha told him.

He couldn't think of anything more to say. It was starting to rain. He stood in the drizzle and watched as the paramedics loaded Bill into the ambulance and Brenda listed all the urgent things she had for Tasha to do.

He'd never felt more helpless in his life.

At last the ambulance drove away. Brenda gave a cheery wave—'See you tomorrow, Tasha!'— and he was left with Tasha.

She returned to his car—to the driving side— climbed in and looked out at him.

'Aren't you getting in?'

He did. He had to use his hands to heave his weak leg into the car and that made him more frustrated still.

'You will go surfing,' she said.

'What?'

'Rhonda and Hilda told me you hit your head on the rocks, surfing. Why don't the Blake boys choose nice safe hobbies?'

'Like macramé.'

'Macramé's good,' she said thoughtfully. 'Though needles can be sharp.'

'Tasha...'

'Yes?' She'd started the car and was heading for home. For his place.

'You shouldn't have come.' It came out as a snap and he winced, but she was smiling, amused rather than offended.

'Of course I should. You need me, but, then, you're a Blake boy so you think you don't need anyone.'

He wasn't sure how to answer that. 'I can't sit back and watch you work.'

'Of course you can't,' she said equitably. 'And you're not going to. Rhonda and Hilda gave me a list of the rehab routine you should be following. The most important thing to do after a head injury is to get your body back to what it was, fast, before the damage can't be reversed. So medical emergencies are for me to deal with, not you.'

He stared. 'You're not bossy!'

'What do you mean, I'm not bossy?'

'When you were here before. You were...'

'Traumatised?' she suggested for him when he didn't come up with a word. 'Of course. That's what I was when you knew me.' Once again her voice gentled. 'But I'm not traumatised now, Tom, and you are. That's what I'm here for. You were my support person. Now I'm yours.'

There seemed nothing left to say. He stared out at the rain-swept road and felt things shift inside him that he'd had no idea could shift.

This was Tasha, a widow, the mother of a baby who'd died. She was battered by life and she'd needed him in the most desperate of circumstances.

Now she was here to help him, but that wasn't what was throwing him. Or not so much. What was throwing him was that she looked...like Susie?

No. She looked nothing like Susie but there was a common thread. The women he dated were beautiful but, more important, they were self-reliant.

Tom Blake didn't need women. He'd trained himself not to need them. He'd seen the heartache his father had caused when he couldn't commit himself to a long-term relationship and Tom didn't trust himself not to do the same. He'd never understood how people committed themselves to a monogamous relationship. He liked people—he liked women—too much.

The women he dated knew it. He was always honest. Cray Point had a limited pool of single women but there were enough. Divorcees. Older women who loved the idea of dating but who'd been burned before. Of course there were women who thought they could change his mind but he was honest from the start.

His mind couldn't be changed and he knew it. He had no intention of hurting anyone as his mother had been hurt. So he stepped back and he never dated anyone he thought was the least bit vulnerable.

That didn't mean he wasn't attracted, though, and the woman beside him now...

Was his stepbrother's widow. Was out of bounds.

Why? She was beautiful. She was competent. She seemed like she was taking over his life as he knew it.

She seemed almost...fun.

That was a weird concept but it was the one that sprang into his mind and stayed. Since the accident his life had been grey, filled with pain and boredom. He hadn't had the energy to keep up with past relationships or start another. But now there was Tasha...

'The first thing we need to decide is where I live,' she told him.

'Where you live... You really intend staying?'

'I told Rhonda and Hilda I'll stay as long as you need me, and one look at you tells me you'll need me for a while.'

'Thanks.'

'Tom, you do need to admit you need help. Your left leg's dragging. There's a faint slur in your voice, and did you know your smile's lop-sided?'

He wasn't smiling now. 'I'm fine.'

'You're not, and without rehab you risk not being fine permanently. You know that. Surely it's just commitment to the medical needs of this town that's stopped you focusing, so I'm not leaving. Rhonda and Hilda say I can use their cottage. They have cats, which their next-door neighbour is currently feeding, and cats make me sneeze, but I'd rather sneeze than interfere with your love life.'

'I don't have a love life.'

'And that was inappropriate. Sorry.' She was serious now. 'Tom, when I stayed with you last year I was shocked and numb and I was very, very grateful, which is why I'm here now. But I'm no longer shocked and numb and if Susie or anyone else is on the scene, or if you simply want privacy... Be honest, Tom. If you'd like me to stay at Rhonda and Hilda's I'll make a deal with the cats. There are two bedrooms. They can have one, I can have the other.'

'Stay with me.' To say he was disconcerted was an understatement and his voice came out a growl, but she smiled.

'So you're happy for me to stay until that limp disappears?'

'I seem to be stuck with you.'

'That's gracious.'

It wasn't but she was looking amused, and that disconcerted him even more.

But he was behaving like a bore. She'd come a long way to help him. He needed to get his act together and be grateful.

'I'm sorry.' He closed his eyes. 'Tell me you haven't messed with your career path or given up your holidays for the next ten years to come here.'

'I haven't.' Her voice softened. 'Tom, I've just reached the end of my contract and to be honest I was thinking of changing workplaces anyway. This gives me time to consider where I'll go next.'

'Back to your work with Médicins Sans Frontières?'

'I'm not sure, but I need to think and Cray Point is as good a place to think as any. Your house, or Rhonda and Hilda's place with cats? It's up to you, Tom, but be honest, if you'd rather I'm out of your hair then Rhonda and Hilda's it is.'

'If you stay at my place you'll boss me,' he said, and that grin flashed out again, the grin he hadn't known she'd possessed until today.

'Of course I will. Exercise, exercise, exercise. I've made a commitment. I'm staying until you're recovered and I can't see myself spending the rest of my life in Cray Point.'

'There are worse places to stay.'

'There are,' she agreed. 'But the problem is that Cray Point comes with a Blake boy and this is messing with another vow. And that's to never have anything to do with anyone resembling a Blake boy ever again.'

'You're labelling me with my brother and father?'

'I surely am,' she said cordially. 'And I intend to keep doing so. Believe me, it's the only safe thing to do. So you can do what you like. Our lives shouldn't mesh—just as long as you do your rehab.'

He lay in bed that night and thought of the gift she'd given him. The freedom to get himself back to normal.

What was normal?

Nothing felt normal any more.

His body had once been what he was. When he'd wanted to move, his body had moved. When he'd wanted to surf, run, put himself in peril hauling people out of crashed cars, make love, his body had come along with him. It had done what he'd demanded of it, no questions asked.

But now it was like his body belonged to one of his patients—not him. Since that night when a blinding headache had suddenly seen him crash, limp, helpless, his body had seemed separate from what he was. The sensation had been terrifying.

What he should have done—and he knew this—was stay away from Cray Point and put his all into rehab. He should be working with his body until it felt like it belonged to him again. Only in some weird way that'd be acknowledging that his damaged body had control, not him. His body would be dictating that he leave Cray Point without a doctor. His body would be dictating what he could and couldn't do.

So he'd hunkered back down in Cray Point. Dating had stopped. Everything had stopped but work while he fought for control again.

And now here was Tasha, proposing a course of action it was sensible to accept but which meant he was out of control again.

He was being dumb. Paranoid. Hers was a magnificent gesture and he should accept it with gratitude. But to calmly sit back and let her take over his life...

That was an overstatement.

He closed his eyes and fought for sleep but it wouldn't come. He felt like he was flailing, almost as helpless as that first day in Intensive Care, when he'd realised his arm and leg wouldn't respond to his commands.

How could Tasha make him feel like that?

Control...

It had been his mantra all his life. He'd seen the emotional mess his father had caused. He'd seen his mother's pain and he'd sworn he'd never cause it and never have it happen to him.

But during these last few weeks his body had shown him how little control he really had, and now Tasha was showing him the same.

'It's dumb to feel like this.'

He said it out loud and it echoed in the darkened room. His body was recovering and with Tasha's help then maybe...no, make that surely, it would recover completely.

All he had to do was let Tasha take control.

All he had to do was let go.

CHAPTER FIVE

SHE WOKE TO the sound of thumping. It wasn't steady, though. It was a decidedly wobbly thump.

Someone was thumping on the veranda outside her bedroom window.

She glanced at her bedside clock and practically yelped. It was after eight. She'd gone to bed over twelve hours ago. Despite the feigned chirpiness she'd put on for Tom, her body had demanded sleep.

Maybe that was a defence.

For now she was here, the place she'd left eighteen months ago, wondering if she could ever forget.

She didn't want to forget, but the pain of remembering was appalling. At least in London she could throw herself into her work, but here...

Up on the headland was a tiny grave. She'd thought she'd go there last night but in the end she just couldn't. She'd declined Tom's invitation to share dinner. She'd pleaded jet lag, eaten eggs on toast and hit the pillows.

But now… Thump…thump…thump…

Intrigued, she tossed back the covers and hauled up the window. Her bedroom looked straight over the veranda to the ocean beyond. The sea air felt blissful. She breathed in the salt and then she looked along the veranda and decided to stop breathing for a while.

The mixed emotions of moments ago came to a grinding halt.

For Tom was here, and Tom was gorgeous.

There was no other word for it. He was totally, absolutely gorgeous.

He was wearing boxers and nothing else. The weak winter sun was doing its best to make his bronzed body glisten. A sheen of sweat on his chest and brow made him look even more…

Gorgeous. She couldn't get past that word.

Tom had a skipping rope and was doing his best to skip, but his lazy leg was dragging. He was forcing himself on, but every second or third skip his leg didn't lift. He'd swear and keep going.

'Good morning.'

Tasha's greeting made him miss the rope again.

She was just along the veranda. She'd stuck her head out the window and she smiled as he turned to look at her.

'What's the sound of a centipede with a wooden leg?' she asked.

'I don't know—what?' he demanded, goaded, knowing something corny was coming.

'Ninety-nine thump,' she told him, and grinned as if it was an entirely original joke and she expected applause. 'That's you, only you don't get to ninety-nine.' She swung her legs over the window sill and perched. She was wearing a long white nightie with lace inserts. It reached her ankles and reminded him of something his grandma would have worn, but there the similarity ended.

Tasha didn't look like anyone's grandma, Tom thought. Her brown-gold curls were tousled from sleep, tumbling to her shoulders. She wore no make-up but she needed none. She looked pert and wide awake and beautiful.

And interested.

'What's causing the leg to drag?' she asked, as if it was any of her business.

'A subarachnoid haemorrhage,' he said carefully. 'Pressure in the brain.'

'I get that, you idiot,' she told him. 'In case

you've forgotten, I have a medical degree, too. So, let me see... Balance problems can be due to muscle weakness and paralysis, damage to the cerebellum—that's the part of the brain that controls balance,' she added kindly. 'You could have loss of sensation in the leg itself, with high-tone or low-tone damage to the vestibular system, though I see no evidence of spasticity. You could have impaired vision, hypotension, ataxia, or poor awareness of body position. You have been assessed?'

'In hospital.' He hated talking of his medical problems—especially to a woman in a night-gown, a woman who until now he'd thought of as someone he could help.

Their roles were suddenly upside down and the sensation made him feel like snapping and retreating.

He couldn't. She'd come here to help. He owed it to her to be cordial, even grateful.

'But not since you came home, which was three weeks ago,' she was saying. 'You have foot-drop. You probably need a brace to support the ankle. Are you having pain?'

'No!'

'I'll bet you get tired. Fatigue is one of the most

common after-effects of what's happened to you, especially if you entertain on the side.'

'I am not tired and I don't entertain!'

'And crabbiness, too,' she said equitably. 'Personality changes. You weren't crabby last time I was here.'

'Tasha…'

'So you need a thorough physiotherapy assessment.' She gave him an almost apologetic smile. 'You know, I'm not the only bossy woman in your life right now. Rhonda was in full organisation mode before I left England. She's determined you make the most of me being here, so she's booked an assessment for you this afternoon. The plan is for me to take your morning clinic and then to drive you to Summer Bay. They have a full physio clinic, with all the rehab equipment you need. They'll do a full assessment and start you this very afternoon. And every afternoon I'm here.'

'What…?'

'Rhonda's set it up and I agreed,' she told him calmly. 'I know you will, too. It's not worth me coming all this way for you to be put on a waiting list.'

'I don't need—'

'Of course you do and you know it.' She softened. 'Tom, you haven't had time to take care of
yourself. I get that, but I'm here now. You know
you need specialised physio, targeted specifically
for your problems. Jumping rope's good but it has
limitations. The Summer Bay clinic has a neuro-
physiotherapist on site and she sounds excellent.
She'll co-ordinate the team.'

'Who told you…?'

'Rhonda explained the situation,' she said. 'You
hired a bossy boots, not me, so you have only
yourself to blame that she's getting us organised.
But you know she's right. Muscle weakness,
speech… Your recovery needs to be a multidis-
ciplinary effort.'

'I don't need…' He was starting to sound like
a parrot.

'You know you do need,' she said patiently.
'You're trying to be your own doctor and it
doesn't work.' Her voice gentled again. 'Tom,
when I hit the wall I knew to come to you for
help. You took over and I let you. I needed to let
you. So now it's you who's in trouble. We can't
make you but why not relax and go with what
Rhonda and Hilda and I have planned?'

'"Blast of the trumpet…"' he managed, and she grinned.

'"Against the monstrous regiment of women"?' She even had the temerity to chuckle. 'John Knox knew what he was up against, although I think it was only two women he was complaining of—the women on the throne. You have three women to rail against—me, Rhonda and Hilda. Now… could you walk me through the clinic work after breakfast? Then you can take a nice nap while I do morning surgery.'

'A nice nap…' He was almost speechless.

'I might need to wake you if there's something I don't understand,' she told him. 'But I hope I won't.'

'Are you really registered to work in Australia?'

'Of course,' she said, sounding wounded. 'I hold an Australian passport and I organised Australian registration and worked here during IVF and the first part of my pregnancy. I know the system. Okay, I'm heading for the shower. Then breakfast. Let's get this show on the road.'

She stood under the shower and let the hot water wash away the cobwebs left from jet lag.

She tried not to shake.

She'd done well, she thought. She'd acted as if she knew what she was doing, as if she was on top of her world.

Except she wasn't. And she wasn't because when all was said and done, Tom Blake was just that. A Blake boy. The sight of his near naked body on the veranda had shaken her as she'd had no intention of being shaken.

Paul Blake had entered her life like a whirlwind, sweeping her off her feet with his love for adventure, his exuberance and his passion. She'd fallen hard and was married before she knew it. Then she'd spent years watching him take crazy risks. Being terrified for him. Not knowing that he was betraying her and he'd been betraying her almost from the start.

In the end she'd realised marriage vows meant nothing. Personal loyalty meant nothing.

Tom seemed kinder and gentler, but in essence he seemed the same. He admitted openly that he loved women—serial women—and he took the same crazy risks Paul had.

Was she being unfair? Was she judging Tom because of Paul?

No. She was judging Tom because of Alice and Susie, and all the Alices and Susies before, all the women he'd chatted about in his newsy emails. Plus the fact that he'd been injured because of a reckless surfing accident.

She was sensible to judge—so why was she shaking?

Because she was vulnerable? Because the sight of him on the veranda had made something twist inside her that frightened her?

Because she didn't trust herself.

'There's no reason to be scared,' she said out loud. 'I have no intention of going down that road again. Besides, he's not the slightest bit interested.'

'But if he was?' She was talking to herself.

'Then I'd run. I'd head to the cats. Much safer.'

'Even if they make you sneeze?'

'Sneezing's harmless,' she told herself. 'As opposed to the Blake boys, who aren't harmless at all.'

Stuck in the corner of the dressing table was the appointment card outlining the details of the booking she'd made the day before she'd left for Australia.

She'd thought—hoped?—she could be brave enough to try again for a baby.

Now she glanced out the window at Tom, who

was still doggedly skipping. She remembered how much she'd needed him.

Fear flooded back.

She picked up the appointment card and thrust it back into the bottom recess of her suitcase.

Her reaction to Tom said that she wasn't very brave at all.

Any doubts as to Tasha's ability to take over were allayed the moment Tom took Tasha into the clinic.

Rhonda and Hilda's niece was currently filling in for Rhonda. To say Millie was less than satisfactory was an understatement. She was cute and blonde and dimwitted. She chewed gum and watched while Tom and Tasha sorted the morning files. There was half an hour before the first patient was due, and Tom had no intention of leaving unless Tasha seemed capable.

She proved it in moments.

He handed her the list of appointments and watched as she did a fast check of the associated files. As she reached the end of the list she turned to him, looking worried.

'Mrs Connor?' she said. 'Margie Connor? Millie's booked her in for last on the list but according to her file her last three appointments have been for serious cardio. events. The reason for today's visit is that her legs are swelling and she's feeling breathless. Should we—?'

And Tom swore and reached for the phone. Rhonda would have picked this up.

'Margie Connor never rings unless it's something major, and her heart failure's getting worse,' he told Tasha. 'Good call.'

Margie answered on the second ring, which was another confirmation that all was far from well. Normally Margie would be on the beach with her dogs at this time of the morning.

'Margie? You're coming in this morning? Millie says it's your legs and you're short of breath?' He listened and grimaced.

'If they're that swollen get Ron to bring you in straight away. Pack a nightie and toothbrush— you know the drill. We might get away with adjusting your medication but if the swelling's too much you could need a couple of days in hospital to get rid of the fluids. It's nothing to panic about but the sooner we see you, the less fluid we'll have to get rid of. I'll be waiting at the clinic. Straight away, Margie. Don't spend time making yourself beautiful for me. You're gorgeous as you are.'

He replaced the receiver and turned and Tasha was glaring at him. Strangely her glare made him want to chuckle. She was like a mother hen, defending her territory.

Only her territory was actually his.

'You aren't staying here,' she said severely. 'I can deal with this.'

'Margie's scared,' he said simply. 'She has grounds for being scared. I'm not having her face a strange doctor.'

'I'm not strange.'

'No,' he said, and he had to suppress a grin as her glare continued. 'You're not. Apologies. But you are different. I need to be here and you need to accept it. Tasha, what you're proposing will only work if you let me share when it's appropriate. It's appropriate now.'

Was it a glare or was it a glower? He couldn't decide, but either way it was cute.

Um…cute wasn't on the agenda. She was a colleague.

He held up his hands, as if in surrender. He wasn't in control. He knew it, he didn't like it but he had to accept it. 'Tasha, I know I've been pig-headed in keeping on working,' he told her. 'But until now I haven't had much choice. I accept I need help. Believe it or not, I'm deeply grateful that you're here and I will do the rehab. Of course I will. But this is my town and these are my people. You need to accept that I care.'

'You're supposed to rest.'

'Rest doesn't mean lying in bed for the next couple of months. We can share. I'll back off when I need to—and, yes, I'll concede you may be a better judge of that than I am—but we have two consulting rooms. I'll work mornings, but at half-pace. You'll work next door and if you need me, call.'

She stood back and considered, while on the sidelines Millie watched on with vague interest. It was like an intellectual decision was being made, he thought. A clinical assessment with a prognosis at the end.

She was very, very cute.

'Okay,' she said at last. 'That seems fair but there's a deal-breaker. In the mornings we share your work. In the afternoons you let me share your rehabilitation.'

That took him aback. 'What do you mean?'

'Just that. You let me come with you this afternoon and hear what the physios say. I have no intention of watching as you complete every exercise, but someone close to you should have an overview. You know patients often hear only what they want or think they need to hear. You don't have a mum and you don't have a partner—unless you're considering taking Millie or Susie. Are you?'

'No!' he said, as Millie recoiled in horror at the idea.

She grinned. 'Then let me in, Tom. You know rehab is gruelling. You'll need encouragement and sometimes you'll need pushing. You need to share.'

'I don't need…'

'You keep saying that, but is it true? You don't need my help? Like Bill didn't need a doctor at the foot of the steps yesterday? Tom, be honest.'

'I don't want to share.' How ungracious was that, but the words seemed to come from deep inside. Handing over to Tasha was losing even more of the control he valued so much.

She raised her brows and gave him a long, hard look. And then she seemed to come to a decision.

'Tom, the way I see it, we have three alternatives. One—you leave everything to me. Two—you share. Three—I leave.'

Things were suddenly serious. 'What the...?'

'I told Rhonda and Hilda I'd take over your workload, whether you want me or not. But of course I can't.'

'It's good of you to see it.'

That earned him a wry smile. 'I am being good,' she told him. 'I'm trying my hardest to see this from your point of view. I'm thinking of you as yet another gung-ho Blake boy, but what you just said has made me brave enough to push my luck. You said, "This is my town. You need to accept that I care." So I accept you care, but—accepting that—do you concede that the town needs me? You can't cope yourself. Do you need me to be here?'

There was a moment's silence. He met her gaze and she met his gaze right back. Her eyes flashed a challenge.

And amazingly he also saw the faintest hint of laughter, as if she knew the dilemma he was in and was faintly enjoying it. Whereas he wasn't.

'Yes,' he said at last, and then added a grudging 'Thank you.'

'And do you also concede that most people dealing with head injuries need a support person?'

'I don't—'

'Concede it,' she said. 'You said it yourself—for now, I may be a better judge than you are. I'm here not only for this town or for your patients. I'm here for your care as well.' The laughter faded. 'Tom, eighteen months ago I realised I needed a support person and I came to you. I followed your advice and you were with me every step of the way. If you were treating someone for a head injury now, would you say they needed to take someone with them for at least the initial assessment at rehab?'

'I don't need...' He stopped. The three words were like a repetitive mantra in his head but the worst thing about this mantra was he knew it wasn't true.

'The Blake boys don't need,' she said, and her voice was suddenly grim. 'Not usually. But for now face the fact that you do. When people are listening to what medical practitioners are telling them their hearing's often limited. They hear the first thing but they're so busy taking it in that they miss the next.'

'I'm a doctor,' he snapped. 'I don't miss things.'

But at that Millie chimed in with something like glee. 'Like the top step yesterday? You missed that. You bruised yourself, too, though you wouldn't let anyone help. And your medical bag.' Millie was enjoying herself. 'On Tuesday you left your bag in the surgery and you had to get the taxi to turn around. You're missing things all the time.'

'I normally leave my bag in my car,' he said through gritted teeth. 'I'm not used—'

'Exactly,' Tasha told him. 'Thank you, Millie. That's just the point. You're not used to any of this. Give up, Tom,' she said, her voice gentling. 'For once, accept that you're human like the rest of us. And I will leave if you don't accept my help.'

'What, go back to England?'

'There are other reasons I need to be in Australia,' she said, diffidently. 'Right now the overriding one is you, but I don't need to be in Cray Point. It's co-operation or nothing.'

'Or you'll go where?'

'What I do from now on is none of your business. Do you want my help or not?'

'I… Yes.' There was nothing else to say.

And she smiled, a smile that held understanding as well as satisfaction. 'Excellent,' she said, and strangely he got the feeling that she understood where he was coming from. 'Is that a car? Could Margie be here already?'

She was, and she was in almost complete heart failure. Medical need took over.

A truce had been reached. Sort of. For a while Tom was able to forget his doubts as he and Tasha fought to stabilise her.

Finally Margie was loaded onto the medevac chopper and evacuated to Melbourne, her prognosis a whole lot better than when she'd arrived. Tom took himself to his room. Tasha took the spare room and they started working through patients.

It was a normal day, Tom told himself. Except that Tasha was in the next room and Tasha was bossy and Tasha was...

Disturbing.

He'd been out of his comfort zone ever since the accident, floundering with loss of control.

Tasha's arrival should have helped, he told himself. So why did he feel even more out of control now than he had before she'd arrived?

* * *

Later that afternoon Tasha drove him across to Summer Bay, while he tried not to grit his teeth beside her.

Tasha didn't mind his silence. The sun had come out. Tom's car was a soft top and she'd asked that they take the roof down. Tom had consented with bad grace but the wind from the sea blew her curls out behind her and she felt like the fog of the last eighteen months was lifting a little.

This really was the most beautiful place. Every curve seemed to open a wilder view of the ocean and the air was so salty she could almost taste it.

The sea was winter wild. She felt clean and refreshed and ready for anything.

Another try at pregnancy?

She thought of the card at the bottom of her suitcase. How much courage would she need to be to go there?

Too much.

Focus on what comes next, she told herself, which was getting Tom through rehab. She glanced across at his grumpy face and smiled.

'You look like a kid heading for the dentist.'

'That's what I feel like,' he admitted. 'You know I can do this on my own.'

'I know you can't.'

'What made you so know-all?'

'A medical degree,' she said serenely. 'Same as you. If you were your patient you'd be saying exactly the same.'

'And my patient would have the right to refuse.'

'He would,' she said equitably. 'And you'd tell him exactly what he'd be losing in the future by doing so.' She considered for a little, and then glanced at him again. 'Tom...would I be right in thinking you're afraid you might fail? That you won't recover the power you once had?'

He didn't reply. The look on his face said she'd nailed it.

'You've come so far,' she said gently. 'Rhonda and Hilda told me how much damage there was, and you've fought back. You know it's still early days. You know...'

'I do know.'

'But the world was yours before and now... You're no longer invincible. But you must have felt like that before. You and Paul and your dad before you. Daring all, and never thinking of the cost.'

'Do you really think—?'

'I know,' she snapped, and then got herself

under control again. 'Sorry. That's past anger from watching Paul go off to climb mountains. And knowing your dad was killed test-driving a car at...what speed? And looking at the damage you've done surfing in stupid conditions. But you will get better, Tom. Every prognosticator tells me you will, so you might as well just get on with it.' She steered the beautiful little car around the next curve and took in the stunning vista before her and then she grinned. 'How often have you been bossed by a woman?'

There was no answer. She tried to suppress her grin and she kept on driving.

How often had he been bossed by a woman? Never?

He'd been raised by a woman who'd been so in love with his father that she'd never got over it. She'd adored her son but her ambitions for herself had disappeared the day her husband had walked out on her. The house had been a shrine to that short marriage. She'd been loving but weak and Tom had learned early that he could pretty much do what he liked.

He loved his mum. He loved Cray Point, but even as a child he'd learned to be deathly afraid of the love that consumed his mother. That kind of love meant misery and heartache and he had no intention of going down that road.

His mother had lost control of her life the moment she'd met his philandering father. To Tom, control was his mantra. He put up with Rhonda and Hilda's bossiness—he even enjoyed it—but theirs was bossiness at the edges. The big decisions in life were his.

He was still in control now, he told himself. He didn't need to accept Tasha's presence at his physiotherapy session. Would she leave if she didn't think he was putting a hundred and ten percent into these sessions?

She may well.

Right now she looked like she was enjoying the sun on her face, the wind in her hair, but underneath her smile was a determination he'd had no clue about.

Had losing Paul and then losing her baby caused that determination, or had it already been there?

'Where do you call home?' he asked, tangentially, and she glanced at him for a moment before turning her attention back to the road.

'Why do you ask?'

'It's just...you went back to England. Is home there?'

'No.' She hesitated. 'I've never really had a home.'

'Never?'

'My mum and dad were with the Australian army but they were based all over the world. They were Special Services, so for half of my childhood I was never allowed to know where they were. When they were killed I was in a boarding school in Sydney but I'd only been there for eighteen months. Before that I'd been in an international school in Egypt. Before that...a list of countries I can hardly remember. After they died I stayed with my aunt in London, but she doesn't like me. I remind her of my mother and it still makes her cry. You can't imagine how wearying that is. But I'm her duty so she's still constantly wondering why I'm not staying with her. I think that's one of the reasons I joined Médicins Sans Frontières where I met Paul. So, no, I don't have a home.'

'If Emily had lived?' It was a hard question but as a doctor he knew that hard questions were too often left unasked.

'I would have made a home,' she said without

missing a beat. 'That was the plan. To settle and stay. To find a community. To give her a child-hood where she could have best friends. And a puppy. She would have loved a puppy.'

Her voice faltered and then she steadied. He knew that about her too, by now. Whatever life threw at her, she steadied.

But he could tell the young Tasha had ached for a puppy.

'But that's the past,' she told him, moving on with a briskness he guessed she'd cultivated from years of deflecting sympathy. 'I need to figure a way forward and I will, but one thing at a time. Next step is to get you working at full capacity. Thus your physiotherapy, and here we are.'

She was his support person.

He'd never imagined he could need such a thing.

A cute, blonde dynamo came out to greet them. 'I'm Dr Sally Myers, neuro-physiotherapist, but I'd prefer it if you called me Sally. Can I call you Tom and Tasha?'

'Of course,' Tasha said. They'd been sitting in the waiting room for ten minutes, with Tom growing more and more impatient while Tasha calmly photographed recipes from housekeeping magazines with her phone. She tucked her phone away as they both rose to greet Sally. 'Tom can see you on his own if he'd like,' she told Sally. 'But would it be more helpful if I came in, too?'

'It always is,' Sally said frankly. 'You'll be needing support, Tom, and if Tasha's happy to give it...'

'Fine,' Tom snapped, and both women looked at him, astonished.

'Sorry,' he muttered. 'It's just that I'm used to doing things alone.'

'Of course you are,' Sally said, sympathetic but firm. 'I'm sure Tasha understands and so do I. But if you don't mind me saying so, you should have been here weeks ago. We have a lot of catching up to do and if Tasha's prepared to help then your chances of a full recovery are greater. Do you want to look a gift horse in the mouth?'

And Tom looked at Tasha and she raised her brows in mock enquiry. She was smiling. Laughing?

Anything less like a horse he'd yet to see.

She was offering him a faster way to recovery. What was he doing, being a bore?

'Let's do it,' he growled.

'So you'd like Tasha to sit in and learn the exercises?' Sally was making him say it out loud.

'Yes.'

And then he glanced at Tasha and her eyes were still dancing. She understood, he thought, and then he thought that if he had to share there was no one he'd rather share with.

She was a loner. She wouldn't push past his boundaries—maybe she even understood them.

'Yes, please,' he said.

He was learning to stand.

It sounded simple. Tasha had been with Tom for almost twenty-four hours now and she'd seen him sit and stand scores of times.

She'd also seen the way he'd favoured his good leg every time.

Sally had assessed him, prepared his programme, told him bluntly what he risked by not doing it, told him the importance of attending clinic every day and then disappeared to deal with the next recalcitrant client. A more junior physiotherapist took over.

She proceeded to have Tom sit and stand and walk, sit and stand and walk, sit, stand and walk. Tom was forced to favour his bad leg every time.

Tasha saw that it hurt. She saw how much of an effort it cost him. She saw the beads of sweat on his forehead and something inside her clenched.

She hated this, and she was forcing him to do it.

No. Her presence let him do it. She knew Tom accepted the need for such hard work. His skipping this morning had shown her how hard he'd been trying himself, but he needed this professional approach.

She was right to have come, even if arriving at Cray Point, being with Tom, being so close to her daughter's grave, did stir up all sorts of emotions she'd rather not face.

Emily...

'Let's end with swimming,' the physio decreed at last. 'Did you bring your swimmers?'

'Yes,' Tasha told her, and Tom swivelled and stared.

'Pardon?'

'Sally told me swimming might be involved. Just lucky I made myself useful with the laundry last time I was here. I knew they were in the laundry cupboard. I brought your boardies rather than the budgie smugglers you wear under your wetsuit.'

'Thanks,' he said through gritted teeth. And

then... 'You know, if you were serious you'd swim with me.'

'I thought you'd never ask,' she told him, and grinned and pulled a pair of rainbow-coloured swimmers from her bag. 'I came here to be a hands-on support person, Tom Blake, and I'm with you all the way.'

Why not? she thought. She'd learned a whole lot about pain in the last eighteen months and one thing stood out. Sitting thinking about it didn't help. She needed to be distracted—and how much more could she be distracted than by jumping into the pool with Tom Blake?

And in the end it was fun. Ridiculously fun. The young physio—Liselle—ran him through some basic water exercises, leg, arm and neck, and then produced a stretchy band, which she used to rope his good arm to his body. Then she turned to Tasha.

'We can do this three ways,' she told them. They were standing chest deep in the warmed pool. 'I can toss a ball back and forth to Tom, making him use his weak arm, while Tasha watches. That's pretty boring. Or, Tasha, I can tape your favoured arm and have you and Tom have a competition as to who can catch the most. But what's most fun is if I play, too. See this neat little net? I get to play goalie. You two work together, both using only your weaker arms. You guys have to stand behind the three-metre line and stay at least two metres apart. The rule is that you need to toss the ball to each other before you aim for goal and it doesn't matter how many times you do it. You feint to try and get the ball past me. Every time you miss I get a point, but every time you work together and get a goal then it's a point to the Wobble Team.'

'The Wobble Team,' Tasha said blankly, and Liselle grinned.

'You're both wobblers, Tom because of your head injury and Tasha because I'm taping your right arm and you'll find even that sets you off balance. Game?'

And Tom and Tasha looked at each other.

'I'm in,' Tasha said. 'Wobblers, huh?'

'No one calls me a wobbler and lives to tell the tale,' Tom growled.

'Prove it, big boy.' Liselle laughed and tossed him the ball.

He caught it and grinned with his success. Too easy. But apparently it was.

'I threw it straight and slowly,' Liselle told him. 'But something tells me you don't like being treated with kid gloves, so sharpen up.'

'Right,' he said, and tossed the ball to Tasha. His arm felt stiff and strange but there was no way he was letting it stop him. 'Let's show this lady what wobblers are capable of.'

And for the first time for six long weeks he had…fun.

It was fun. Yes, his body still didn't feel as if it belonged to him. He had two disadvantages— one was that he was forced to use his weak arm and the other was that his movement was restricted because his leg didn't obey orders the moment he sent it. And Liselle was good. 'I play water polo,' she admitted. 'And, yes, state level.'

But he had Tasha, and Tasha was amazing.

She looked amazing. Her costume wasn't anything to write home about—a simple one-piece— but it was in a myriad of tropical colours. She was trim and lithe and agile, and she ducked and weaved in the water as if water was her second home. She hadn't tied her curls back. She was soaked the first time he threw an awkward ball to her and she dived for it. She surfaced laughing, her curls spiralling every which way, and she tossed the ball back to him and he was so distracted that he missed.

He didn't get that distracted again. Her look of disappointment at his easy miss had him focusing, and she was, too. She was laughing, diving, yelling to him, feigning tosses towards goal, pretending to toss towards the goal and then tossing to him, pretending to toss to him and then tossing straight at the goal.

For all her laughter she was taking this game very seriously. So did he and at the end of half an hour, when Liselle called time, the score was dead even and even Liselle was looking exhausted.

'I need to find you guys a greater handicap,' she told them. 'You work too well together as a team. Tasha, if you keep working Tom like this we'll have him a hundred percent in no time. Will you come to every session?'

'There may be medical imperatives that stop me coming,' Tasha told her. 'But I'll try. And I do the driving so unless Tom wants to catch a taxi I need to bring him.'

Did he want to catch a taxi?

He looked at Tasha, who was swinging herself out of the pool. Water was streaming from her

curls, running in rivulets down the smooth surface of her throat and the curve of her breasts.
Her legs were perfect—no, make that everything
about her was perfect.

No, he didn't want a taxi.

'I think we could do this until we get to the
stage where it's Liselle and me against you, and
we play until we lose,' she told him. 'You reckon
we could do that in two months?'

'There's a challenge,' Liselle said, grinning. 'I
could bring in the rest of my polo team as rein-
forcements.'

And for the first time since the accident Tom
suddenly felt normal. These women were smiling at him, daring him, challenging him. And
they were expecting him to get back to normal
or better.

'You think I can do it?' he demanded, facing
his fears front on.

'I'm sure of it,' Liselle said. 'Look how far
Tasha's driven you today.'

'It was you,' Tasha said.

'It was all of us,' Liselle admitted. 'But, Tom,
with Tasha driving you, there are no limits to
what you can do. I know it.'

* * *

'There are no limits to what you can do.'

The words kept playing in her head, a mockery. It was almost dusk. The sun was sinking in the west. Tom was fast asleep in front of the fire. For all his protestation that he'd coped well, the rehab had knocked him around. While he slept Tasha finally found the time and the courage to walk up the headland to the Cray Point cemetery. To Emily's grave.

It was a place of tranquil beauty, overlooking the sea. Emily's grave was a simple headstone surrounded by carefully cultivated flowers.

Planted by Tom.

She had so many conflicted emotions they were playing havoc with her mind.

Tom. Being here. Grief.

Trying for another baby.

To have another baby feeling as she did wasn't fair, she thought. She was still gutted by Emily's death. The pain and humiliation she'd received from Paul was still with her, and yet she hadn't managed to build defences.

For that was what was bothering her most now. She knew she could fall for Tom. His very smile seemed dangerous.

'So how weak does that make me?' she asked Emily, as she crouched by the little grave and ran her fingers through Tom's flowers.

She hadn't been strong enough for Emily. She'd needed Tom. 'And something keeps whispering that I still need him,' she said out loud, whispering to her little girl. 'How can I think of another baby without the strength to face whatever comes?'

There are no limits to what you can do...

'Maybe there are,' she told herself. 'And maybe I've reached them. I loved Mum and Dad. I thought I loved Paul, and, oh, I loved you, my Emily. But each time... How can I think of trying again?'

But it wasn't just the thought of another baby that had her asking the question.

Tom... How she felt, seeing him again...

It was weakness.

But for some reason the question kept hammering in her brain.

How could she think of trying again?

CHAPTER SIX

LIFE SETTLED INTO a routine—sort of—but a medical house was never normal. As soon as the locals realised Tasha was available, the phone went all the time.

'Do you spend all your time in the clinic?' Tasha demanded at the end of the second week. She'd just finished an extra clinic and Tom had come to find her.

'I can't,' Tom told her. 'We have a huge elderly population. I need to do house calls.'

But Tasha was doing the house calls now, and was astounded by how many were needed. 'You need two permanent doctors,' she told him.

'We do. Are you interested?'

He'd just returned from a long rehab session to which he'd had to go alone. Ray Desling had spilt his toe with an axe just as they'd been preparing to leave. It had nearly killed Tom to climb into a taxi and leave Tasha to clean and stitch, but her threat was still there.

'*You stop doing rehab, I stop being here.*'

What was he doing? Proposing she stay? For ever?

'What would I do in Cray Point?' she asked, sounding astounded.

'Live?' He limped behind the reception desk so he could see the files she was processing. It felt good to stand beside her at the end of the day, figuring how much they'd achieved. That included how much he'd achieved. The left-sided weakness was lessening by the day.

'Live?' she said now, sounding puzzled. 'Just live?'

'Like everyone else,' he told her. 'That's what we do in Cray Point. You could learn to surf and fill your spare time patching people up. That's the story of my life.'

'With ladies on the side,' she retorted. 'Which reminds me, I've been here for two weeks and nary a lady. Is there a problem?'

He managed a smile. Since his accident he hadn't felt the least bit like dating. In truth, ever since Emily's death his heart hadn't been in it, and maybe the women he'd spent time with sensed it. But he wasn't telling Tasha that.

'Susie's tossed me over for the guy who fixes her computer,' he told her, and tried to look glum.

'Really?'

'Really.'

'Are you heartbroken?'

He forgot the glum and grinned. 'How can I compete with someone who knows how to increase internet speed? In times gone by, legend says women found doctors sexy but I suspect they only found them useful. Geekiness now seems a strong draw card.'

'I'm sorry.'

'Don't be. I don't get involved. I never have.'

'Because?'

'Because I suspect I'm like my father and my brother,' he said honestly. 'I have no idea how to play happy families and I suspect it's too late to learn. Now, about you staying...'

'You're offering me a job?'

'If you're interested.'

'I'm not,' she said, too quickly.

'Then I guess it's my turn to ask: because?'

'Same reason. Because I suspect you're like your father and your brother.'

He frowned. 'Tasha, I'm offering you a job, not proposing marriage.'

'That's right,' she agreed. 'You are. But working together... It couldn't work long-term. I don't know if you're aware of the tensions...'

And of course he was. He'd have to be an insensitive idiot not to feel them, but to talk about them out loud...

They'd been in the same house for two weeks now and the tensions she'd talked of were building. There was nothing tangible, just an undercurrent of awareness that couldn't be avoided.

It was a big old house with a rabbit warren of rooms, yet somehow he always knew where Tasha was. When she walked into the room, tension escalated. When they cooked together, when their bodies brushed in passing, or sometimes at sunset when he sat on the veranda and she came out to join him, the tension was so great it felt almost a physical thing.

It wasn't helped by the physio sessions. The water play was something he looked forward to more and more. He'd felt almost gutted today when Tasha hadn't been able to come. He loved her skills and her excitement. He loved the way she beamed whenever he pushed himself to the limit and achieved more and more.

So what? She was a friend, not a lover. There was no reason for tension.

She was a woman without a home, without a base. She was a fully qualified medical practitioner. A colleague. It was entirely sensible to be offering her a job.

But she'd been feeling the tension, too, and the knowledge set him aback.

'It's hormonal,' he said, trying to sound knowledgeable, trying to set things on a medical footing. 'Two single adults, working closely together... But there's nothing between us...'

'There's a whole lot between us, but attraction isn't possible.'

'No?'

'No,' she said flatly. 'You need to find yourself another Susie.'

'That sounds insulting.' He thought about it for a little longer. 'It sounds like you're afraid.'

'I'm not afraid,' she told him. 'And I didn't mean to be insulting. But I'm aware, and I don't want to stay aware. I don't intend to feel that tension for the rest of my life.'

'Hey, we're adults,' he said, striving for lightness. 'Surely we can get over a bit of physical attraction.'

'Is that what it is?'

'You're hot,' he said honestly.

'Like Susie and Alice and the rest.'

'Tasha…'

'Too right, it's insulting,' she said flatly. 'Don't you ever call me hot again. This is an inappropriate conversation to be having with a colleague, which demonstrates my point. We can't be colleagues. I leave in six weeks. You'll be fit enough to drive again and take over here. I'll get on with my life.'

'What will you do?'

'I have plans.'

'Care to share?'

'No.' How could she talk to Tom about what she'd hardly faced herself? What she probably didn't have the courage to face.

'Because you don't know?'

'I'm a doctor. I can go anywhere I want in the world and get a job.'

'Drift, you mean.'

'It's better than staying here and being seduced by you.'

Silence.

The words hung. And hung and hung.

Tasha closed her eyes. *Beam me up, Scottie,* she thought. What had she just said?

'I wouldn't,' Tom said at last in a voice that didn't sound like his own. 'I have no intention—'

'I know. I'm sorry. I have no idea where that came from.'

Another silence. And then...

'Because we both want it?' Tom asked.

She covered her face with her hands. 'No.'

'Why not?'

'This is a reaction from not having a Susie or someone like her around,' she whispered into her hands. 'It reflects badly on both of us.'

'It has nothing to do with Susie. It's the way you make me feel.'

'Then don't feel. We both know it's impossible.'

'Why is it impossible?'

'Because I have no intention of being one of your brief flings and you don't know how to do anything else. You've said it yourself. And me... I have no intention of being involved with another Blake boy.'

'I'm not Paul.'

'You're not, but you're like him in so many ways. I have no idea why he married me. He managed to stay by my side for our honeymoon but that was the extent of it. Then he was off adventuring, challenging himself, pushing himself to the limit. Heaven knows if there were other women. I only found out about the last, but looking back, he made our lives so separate there may well have been others.'

'So why did you marry him?'

'Who knows?' She shrugged. 'Maybe he reminded me of my parents. Maybe I'm genetically drawn to risk-takers, or maybe I'm just stupid. Persuading me to marry him must have seemed a challenge to Paul, but once the challenge was met he moved on. For a time I tried to keep up. I learned to abseil and we climbed in places I still can't believe. I went caving and scuba diving, and we did it in some of the most dangerous countries in the world. I pushed myself to the limit but pretty soon I realised that no matter what I did I wasn't important to him. It was the thrill of conquering that was important. And finally I discovered that included women... Who needed a wife? There could always be another Susie or another Alice.'

'That's not fair.'

'To who?'

'To me. I'm not Paul.'

'Of course you're not,' she agreed. 'But you said yourself you don't know about being faithful. And then there's the fact that you threw yourself onto rocks in the surf on a day everyone knew it was stupid to be there.'

'I—'

'Please, Tom,' she said wearily. 'This is a dumb conversation. I never meant to say those things and I regret it already. I'm being rude and judgemental and I have no right to be either. I'm sorry. It's my problem, not yours, but it is a problem and it means I can't stay. So can we just go back to how we were fifteen minutes ago? I have Emma Ladley bringing her daughter in any minute. Megan has menstrual problems, which Emma thinks have been compounded by boyfriend woes. Women's business. You need to leave.'

'You don't need me?'

'Of course I don't need you,' she managed. 'I needed you once and I'm very grateful but I have no intention of needing you again.'

'Tasha, the job…we could help each other.'

'We could destroy each other,' she told him. 'Please… Leave me be.'

He left and she shook, which was an entirely inappropriate reaction. She'd overreacted to the

point of ridiculous, she told herself. Tom had offered her a job and suddenly they'd been talking
about lust. They'd even talked of the impossibility of a long-term relationship, which was something neither of them had even thought of.

Except she had considered it. Of course she
had. She'd been living with Tom for two weeks
now and she'd been aware of him every moment.
She'd acknowledged the attraction and she hadn't
been able to put it aside.

Tom was her friend. He'd helped her at a time
when she had been most vulnerable. She even
acknowledged that she loved him—as a friend.

Except it wasn't quite as a friend, for every
time he was near her, her body reacted in a way
that was entirely inappropriate. She loved being
near him. Tension or not, she loved sitting out
on the veranda late at night and having him sit
beside her. She loved his body in the pool, the
vulnerability he exposed during rehab, the way
he pushed himself to the limit and the exultation when he achieved the next step in physical
fitness.

She loved the way he locked his gaze with hers
as they passed the ball in their weird version of

water polo. They were getting harder and harder to beat.

They were becoming a team.

'But only for now,' she muttered. 'It's transient. Long-term? No and no and no.'

But living here...

The thought was suddenly like a siren song. Living in Cray Point? Buying her own little cottage? Maybe taking courage in both hands, taking up that appointment for another attempt at IVF, using here as a base...?

Tom was her friend and she knew by now that she could depend on him. She could surely live here, work here, with Tom in the background.

She couldn't because she felt...

'Like I have no intention of feeling,' she muttered. 'Like I'd be nuts to feel. You don't need to take risks—you know where that gets you. Get on with your life, Tasha Raymond, and go and greet your next patient. She has women's troubles and boyfriend troubles. Who needs either? Not me, that's for sure.'

Tom went home and pulled a casserole out of the freezer. How many casseroles had Hilda left? He stared at it for a long moment and then replaced it.

He rang for the taxi.

Five minutes later the taxi pulled up. Karen, the local cab owner, greeted him with cheer.

'Hey, Doc. Got an emergency?' In truth, Karen had been enjoying being on call for him. Until Tasha had arrived she'd been making a fortune.

'I need to go to the supermarket.'

She raised her eyebrows. 'Really? I thought Hilda had organised you everything. Casseroles, pies, deliveries twice a week. When she left she told me you wouldn't need for anything.'

'I don't always need what Hilda thinks. I want a change for dinner tonight.'

'Something special? I heard Susie's going out with Donald. Hmm...' She grinned. 'I'm guessing...you and Tasha...'

'Karen!'

'Just saying.'

'I'm only buying steak!'

'Whatever you say, Doc,' she said expansively. 'Whatever you say.'

Tasha arrived back at the house half an hour later to find the house empty. Her footsteps echoed on the ancient floorboards.

It felt strange. Wrong.

'How fast have I got used to company?' she demanded of herself. Too fast. Apart from her brief, disastrous marriage she'd been a loner all her life, yet here she was reacting with a shiver of desolation because Tom wasn't home.

She walked out to the veranda and the table was set. Two places.

Candles. Flowers.

She'd seen this set-up before, on that appalling night she'd arrived, eighteen months ago.

She'd hardly registered then but she did now. He must have had a date.

Did he think he had a date now?

'You idiot,' she said out loud and, she wasn't sure whether she was talking to herself or to Tom. She'd have an egg on toast later, she told herself. By herself. And then she'd go to bed early.

She didn't need this tension between them and she had no intention of escalating it.

But she couldn't settle. She needed a walk and she knew where she wanted to go.

Five minutes later she was walking along the cliffs, up towards the headland.

Emily was waiting, and tonight of all nights it seemed imperative to talk to her.

* * *

His car was back. That meant Tasha was home—
except she wasn't.

Her coat was missing from the back veranda,
as were her walking boots.

She was upset and that upset him. He still didn't
understand what had happened this afternoon.
All he knew was that he'd messed with their relationship and it felt bad.

He took his gear into the kitchen and set it out.
Salad, steak, fruit and cream. It wasn't nearly as
professional as the meals Hilda had prepared,
but for some reason tonight it felt important to
cook himself.

In truth, he wasn't sure what he was doing. The
ground under him felt shaky and it wasn't just
his weak leg that was the cause.

He opened an excellent wine. He checked the
dining table on the veranda and decided to ditch
the candles and flowers. Then he put them back
again.

Then he ditched them again, dumping them
in the trash so he couldn't change his mind. He
brought the place settings into the kitchen and
set the table there.

Better.

She still wasn't home.

The night was mild and clear. The moon was just coming up, hanging low over the eastern sky. The sounds of the surf and the call of distant plovers were the only things that cut the silence.

He thought of putting on music and decided not to.

What was he doing? He should be getting things back to a normal setting, except he wasn't sure what a normal setting was any more.

Why had he asked her to continue to work here, and why had it escalated so fast?

He headed back out to the veranda. He knew where she'd be. He'd watched her walk up there many times since she'd arrived. There was a tiny grave...

He should let her be. Her time with Emily was not his to share.

But tonight he needed to share. He'd messed with something deeply important. Friendship?

Something more?

She'd made it quite clear she didn't want more and he didn't either.

Or did he?

How could he? The last thing he wanted was to hurt her. How could he promise not to?

He should leave her be. He should...

He didn't. He shrugged on his jacket and took the walking pole he kept beside the door. His leg wasn't up to climbing the headland without support and he had no intention of becoming Tasha's patient.

What did he want?

He didn't know. All he knew was that he was out the door, walking towards the headland with the intention of finding out.

'Should I run?'

She'd lost Emily eighteen months ago but she'd spoken to her every day since she'd lost her.

'You never completely lose a child.' A midwife had told her that, some time in the dark days as Emily had slipped away. 'A baby is part of you. You may lose her from your body but she's carved a space inside you and that space will always be hers.'

She hadn't believed it then. In those appalling first few months, all she'd felt had been an aching, searing loss that threatened to destroy her. But always at the back of the pain had been the slip of comfort, the remembrance of Emily in her arms, the sweet smell of her, the sensation of tiny fingers curving around hers.

And they'd stayed with her. Even back in England she'd felt them, and she'd known that Emily was still real, still a part of her life. So she'd talked to her, and now, high on the headland in Cray Point's tiny cemetery where Emily lay buried, her little girl seemed closer than she'd been since she'd lost her.

'I'm making a mess of things,' she told her. 'I came back because Tom needed me and I owed him.' She took a deep breath. 'The problem is, I'm scared of how I'm feeling.'

And there it was, out there, the thing she was most afraid of.

Surely she couldn't. She'd have something deeply wrong with her to fall for another Blake boy.

She made herself think back to those appalling last few weeks with Paul. They'd had plans to go on vacation to Sardinia. After a gruelling two years of dreadful marriage, she'd clung to it with a final despairing hope.

Not only would it be a fabulous vacation, she'd told herself. It would also be a chance to patch up a marriage that was in real trouble.

And start a baby?

But then Paul had burst back into their apartment, beaming with excitement. 'Change of plans, sweetheart. It's the chance of a lifetime. There's an Australian team heading for Everest next month and someone's dropped out. They've offered me the chance and I can't say no. I know we planned Sardinia but you could come to base camp, do a few easy walks while you wait for me. Tasha, this is amazing...'

'You're not experienced enough,' she'd managed, stunned, and he'd turned angry.

'I'm fit. I've done enough climbing to know the basics. I can do this. I'll need to head back to Australia to organise visas and the like. I still have the apartment in Melbourne and the team will be leaving from there. You can come with me if you want. Stay in Australia or come to base camp.' And then, as she'd said nothing, he'd turned away. 'It doesn't matter. Support me or not, babe, I don't care.'

And then had come the phone call late at night, the call where she'd unashamedly stood in the dark and listened as her husband had talked to his lover.

'She's not coming to base camp—I knew she

wouldn't. She'll stay in Melbourne. That means we can spend a few days in Nepal before we go. Yeah, it means we cut acclimatisation short, but you and me, babe... Everest together and the rest. You just need to peel off that husband and get your act together. Yeah, sweetie, love you, too.'

She hadn't confronted him. She'd been too empty, too sad and shocked. She'd gone to Melbourne with him and helped him pack, all the time thinking this needed to be the last goodbye.

And then the day before he'd left he'd come back to the apartment looking triumphant.

'It's all fixed. I've been to the IVF place and made a deposit. I know you want a baby, sweetie, so if anything happens to me you can still have your baby. You can go to Sardinia, lie on the beach and dream of me.'

She hadn't gone to Sardinia and when the call had come to say Paul and his other 'sweetie' had perished, the emptiness inside her had hardly grown deeper.

She'd thought she loved him.

'What do I know about love?' she asked Emily, and there was no answer.

There were seaside daisies growing around the edges of the cemetery. It was almost dark but the

daisies were white and easy to see. She gathered
handfuls and piled them around the edges of the
little grave, and then sat there, soaking in the silence, trying to make her jumbled thoughts line
up.

She was in so much trouble.

She should leave.

She couldn't leave. She'd promised.

'I'll move to Hilda and Rhonda's house,' she
told Emily. 'It makes sense. Even if the cats make
me sneeze, they can't be as dangerous as Tom.'

'I'm not dangerous.'

She jumped and when she came back to earth
Tom was right beside her. He'd emerged from the
dusk like a shadow. He stood in his dark coat,
leaning on his cane, surveying her with concern.
'Tasha, don't make this bigger than it is.'

'I… What?'

'Me,' he told her. 'You sound afraid and I can't
bear it.'

'I'm not afraid of you.' Except she was.

'Should I go away again?' he asked. 'I don't
want to disturb you.'

'You're not.' That was another lie. But he was
here and he was Tom and there were things she
needed to say.

'Thank you for doing this,' she whispered. Because there was no concrete slab over Emily's grave as there was over most other graves. Instead, there was a rim of sea-tough plants, carefully chosen to create a tiny island of protection from the blast of the sea winds. Within that island were flowers, Hellebores at the moment, Christmas roses, flowers that would bloom in midwinter. And when Tasha had dug down to pull a recalcitrant weed she'd found daffodils bulbs ready to spring to life in late winter, and what looked like tiny ranunculi and anemone bulbs for spring.

Tonight she'd set her daisies at the rim of the grave where there was a space, but she knew instinctively that when she hadn't been here, that space would have been filled by Tom. He'd been tending her baby's grave and the thought did something to her heart she couldn't understand.

Sense or not, she had no defence against Tom's caring.

And he was caring still. 'I'm sorry I upset you,' he said gently. 'It's the last thing I intended.'

'It was me,' she said. 'I had no business to turn a professional proposition into something more.'

'You don't want it to be more?'

'No.'

'I guess that's good,' he told her. 'Because, as you say, I'm a Blake and I didn't learn relationships.'

'You do a nice line in caring despite it,' she told him, carefully focusing her attention on rearranging her daisies. 'I love you for what you've done for us. For what you've done for Emily. But what's between us... It must be because of Emily. We were thrown into a hothouse of emotions. It's hardly surprising we're in a place now we don't recognise.'

'I guess that's right.

He stood back a little, saying nothing more, while she knelt beside Emily's grave and tried to get her emotions under control.

Let him think it's all about Emily, she told herself, but she knew it wasn't.

Finally she stood, brushed herself down and turned to look out at the moonlit sea. There was a long silence, a silence, though, that didn't feel uncomfortable. It was more...peace.

'Thank you for sending me the photographs,' she said at last. 'I... I'm sorry I couldn't respond... the way you deserved for sending them but they were important to me. I loved your emails, too. It sort of meant, even though I'd left, I hadn't abandoned her. She was with a friend.'

'That's quite a compliment.'

'It's the way I feel. But I couldn't write back.'

'I understood.'

'I know you did,' she whispered, and then there was more silence.

And then: 'Would you ever think about another baby?' Tom asked.

The peace was shattered. It was as if the question had opened a locked door, and the space behind was so flooded with emotion that she almost staggered.

But Tom was beside her. He touched her arm, a simple gesture of friendship, and the chaos settled a little.

'Don't answer if you don't want to,' he said, but he was probably the one person in the world who deserved an answer.

'I don't think I'm brave enough.'

'But you want...'

'I don't think I can want.'

He didn't reply. His hand still rested on her arm, and the contact helped. They stood side by side, looking out over the sea while she tried to think of where to take this. While she tried to think of where to take her life?

'So you don't want to stay here,' Tom said at last. 'And you don't think you can try for another baby? What do you want, Tasha?'

Why did the question seem so huge? Why did it seem so impossible?

'Medicine's good,' she said at last, gripping to the one thing that had stayed constant. 'I'm needed.'

'Medicine can't fill your life.'

'Does it fill yours?'

'In a way, yes,' he said simply. 'But medicine for me is more than caring for the next person who comes in the door. My medicine's all about caring for this community. Cray Point took care of me as a kid. It fills something inside me that I can give something back.' He hesitated and then forged on and she sensed he was warring with himself as to whether to say it or not. But then he said it. He asked it.

'What fills that void inside you, Tasha Raymond?'

And it was all she could do not to sob. For there was such a gaping wound inside…

She should be used to it. For heaven's sake, it

had been with her all her life. Her parents had practically abandoned her at birth, leaving her with one carer after another. Then—and psycho-analysts would have a field day with this, she thought grimly—she'd fallen for a guy who'd been just like her parents. A man who'd said he loved her and had then betrayed her.

And then there was Emily.

The hole inside her wasn't diminishing. She couldn't fill it with work and it seemed to be get-ting bigger every day.

But she couldn't fill it here, not with this man, not with this place. And not with another baby?

She'd run out of courage.

'You would find the courage,' Tom said gently, and astonishingly it was as if he'd followed her train of thought. 'Tasha, I've cared for mums who've lost babies. In ten years of general prac-tice I've seen it enough to know how massive that loss is.'

'Tom…'

'I've also seen it enough to sense that moving on is the hardest thing in the world,' he kept on. 'Having another baby seems impossible. But it's the thought that hurts, not the baby that comes. You know you can't ever replace Emily—why would you want to?—but the heart expands. There'll always be a hole where Emily should be, but it can't stop you living. It can't stop you searching for joy and accepting joy when you find it.'

'Tom, I can't...'

'I know,' he said simply, and he touched her cheek, lightly, the faintest of brushes. 'But if you ever feel you can and you need help to find the courage...Tasha, I accept that you can't stay here. I accept we have a relationship that causes you pain. But I'll always be here for you, Tasha. In the background. Egging you on every way I know how.'

'Th-thank you.'

'Think nothing of it,' he said, striving for lightness. He managed a smile. 'I can't do families myself but, wow, I'm good at giving advice. But now... Time to go home?'

And there was nothing else to say. She nodded mutely and turned towards the path.

Tom fell in beside her. His words kept echoing in her head. She needed space to think about them. She needed space to think about what she was feeling.

About a baby?

About Tom.

They walked on in silence. She hardly needed to slow her steps to pace his now. With his cane he was almost as sure as she was on the rough path. He was improving so fast.

Maybe she wouldn't need to stay for six weeks.

The thought was suddenly a desolate one.

But even as she thought it, his weak leg struck a tree root and he stumbled. Not enough to fall but enough for her to instinctively reach out and catch his hand. And hold.

He swore. She knew he hated showing weakness, hated being dependent—but he didn't pull away. His fingers linked through hers with a strength and warmth that made her feel...like she had no business feeling.

Maybe he did need her.

But the Blake men didn't need, and he was a Blake.

Stop it, she told herself. Stop categorising him. He's just Tom.

Just Tom? That was a thought that almost made her laugh. He was so much more than just Tom.

His hand still linked to hers and it felt right. It felt good.

She found herself thinking of the pseudo water-polo games they played, where they teamed against Liselle. Where their gazes stayed almost constantly locked as they fought for a strategy to get the ball through. She loved those games. She'd hated missing this afternoon.

It was fun, but it was more than that. She and Tom were working as a team. They had no hope of scoring a goal by themselves.

Tom was better in the water than she was, stronger, more agile, a better swimmer when he wanted to move fast, but he was handicapped with a weak arm and leg.

He needed her.

On her own she had neither the ability nor the strength to get the ball through the goal net. She needed Tom.

Why did that mesh with the feeling of his hand holding hers?

Why was that thought such a tantalising siren song? To need. To be needed.

'Friends,' Tom said softly as they reached the final rise before the house.

And she thought, Yes. To lose his friendship would break her heart.

But then…friends?

She wanted more.

No. It was her body that wanted more. Her head said it was ridiculous, that she needed no one, that she'd been solitary forever and it was far, far safer that way.

She'd learned life's lessons the hard way, and she had no choice but to accept them.

CHAPTER SEVEN

BY THE TIME they reached the house she almost had herself under control again. Tom unlatched the gate and he had to release her hand while he did. It was the natural time to let go. Friends would have let go then. He no longer needed her support.

He hadn't been holding her hand for support, though, a little voice whispered. Men and women didn't hold hands unless…

Stop it, her head commanded. There's no point thinking like this.

'I have steak for dinner,' Tom said, sounding proud of the concept.

And she thought of the table set on the veranda with the candles and the flowers and she mentally closed down.

'Can you freeze one?' she asked. 'I'm not hungry.'

'You don't want my steak? I was hoping to show off my prowess?'

'You have prowess?' He'd sounded wounded. *Prowess?*

'Hilda's filled my freezer with enough casse-roles to keep me going until Armageddon so it's really hard to show off my splinter skills.'

'Your splinter skills being steak.'

'And salad. Until you've seen me toss a salad you haven't lived.'

And despite herself she chuckled, but then she thought of the candles and the flowers and her laughter faded.

'Not a good idea, Tom.'

'Not?' They were taking off their jackets in the hallway. He flicked on the hall lights and they lit the veranda as well. She glanced at the table she'd seen earlier.

The candles were gone. So were the flowers. The beautiful table setting had disappeared.

He followed her gaze.

'I'm not trying to add you to my list of serial women,' he told her, and she choked.

'Honestly, Tom, to admit you have such a thing...'

'Well, I do,' he said honestly. 'There are some lovely women in this town. I enjoy their company and they seem to enjoy mine. Take Susie. She's just been through a messy divorce. She has two teenage children who run her ragged. She hardly has any time for Susie but for a while she came here, dressed to the nines, ready for a night out. I put an effort into making dinner great and we enjoyed our nights.'

'Your whole nights,' she said before she could stop herself, and he grinned.

'Tasha, I'm no virgin,' he told her. 'But I've always been honest. No strings. I'm good at figuring how far we can take things before anyone gets hurt.'

'You're sure of that? How do you know Susie isn't secretly nursing a broken heart?'

'Hey, Susie called it quits, I didn't. She's in love with her geek.'

'So no one's ever broken their heart over you?'

'That's how my life's designed,' he said. 'That's what happened to my mother. I won't be responsible…'

So that was that. Another irresponsible Blake.

But she stood in the hallway and the space was a bit too narrow. His body was brushing against hers, and at every touch her nerve endings were sending sparks from her toes to her head and back again.

Move on, she told herself harshly, and headed for the kitchen.

She swung open the door and stopped.

The kitchen table was covered with a simple gingham tablecloth. There was the plain cutlery Tom's grandmother must have used, ancient bone-handled knives and forks. Plain crockery, mismatched, some of it cracked and worn.

No flowers. No candles. A bowl of salad sat on the bench and it was a pretty ordinary bowl of salad. Lettuce, tomatoes, cucumbers.

The fire stove at the far end of the kitchen was sending out its gentle warmth. Apart from a gleaming microwave and modern toaster, this room looked like it hadn't changed in a hundred years.

She'd sat here in the days after Emily had died, with Hilda fussing around her and Tom checking in and out to make sure she was okay. She'd hardly noticed the kitchen then, but when she'd returned it had seemed…like coming home? Now it seemed to fold itself around her like a warm cloak. Tom was ushering her in, opening the refrigerator, producing two steaks in a bowl.

'I've made a red wine marinade with an excellent shiraz,' he told her. 'I used half a bottle, which means there's only two glasses left. One for me because that's all I'm permitted. One for you because the last thing I want you to think is that I'm setting the scene for seduction. So, Tasha, steak and salad with me, or are you really intending to go hungry while I hop into both steaks?' And then he grinned and raised an eyebrow in mock enquiry. 'Dare you,' he said. 'Live dangerously. Steak and a glass of wine. What can possibly go wrong?'

If only you knew, Tasha thought helplessly. Oh, Tom, if only you knew.

But she had no choice. She sat and Tom produced an apron with a picture of a monster steak on the front.

'It's my recipe,' he told her, tying his apron strings with a flourish, and she had to grin. The apron read:

Rare: One Beer
Medium: Two Beers
Well Done: Three Beers

It broke the ice and she found herself relaxing a little. The frying pan started to sizzle and Tom had a flash of gourmet inspiration and started frying onions. He added the steak and she was suddenly starving. The smell filled the room and she thought…

Home is where the heart is?

It was an insidious thought, a siren song. Tom had his back to her. He was wearing jeans and a T-shirt, and his T-shirt was a touch too tight. It stretched over his pecs, delineating a build that could send any woman's heart rate up. His neck was sexy, too, she thought idly. It was a good neck. Broad. Strong. He hadn't had a haircut for a while, so the line where his hair started wasn't clearly defined. She could run her fingers up and trace…

Um…not. She poured herself water and then headed for the refrigerator and found herself some ice. It'd be better to pour it over her head, she thought, but she was a sensible woman so she sat and drank it and then concentrated on marshalling her thoughts into some sort of disciplined order. By the time he put a plate of sizzling steak in front of her and sat before her with his, she almost had herself under control.

And then he smiled and her control was shot to pieces again. He poured her wine and she tasted it and it was gorgeous. The night was gorgeous, the steak was gorgeous and Tom was even more gorgeous, and she thought what had this guy been thinking when he'd decided he needed candles and flowers?

'How did you and Liselle go today?' she asked, feeling a bit desperate, hoping to get the conversation to a level where she could operate without her hormones charging in and taking over.

'We did fine motor skills with my left hand,' he told her. 'We put little pegs into little holes until I started going crazy. Then we moved onto the really exciting stuff—we played marbles. You wouldn't believe the adrenalin rush.'

She chuckled, but her heart twisted yet again. Since she'd arrived he hadn't complained—not once. She knew his clumsiness was driving him crazy. She knew there were so many small things that he couldn't do. Even now, cutting his steak was a challenge. His right hand was fine but his stiff left hand didn't hold the way he needed to hold. There was a reason Hilda had left him so many casseroles.

He wouldn't have tried eating steak in front of his myriad women friends, she thought with sudden intuition. But he was cutting his steak in front of her, and she knew by doing it he exposed a vulnerability he hated.

And suddenly she felt herself close to tears.

He was different, she thought. She'd categorised him as a Blake boy but maybe she was wrong. Maybe...

The phone rang.

'Steakus Interruptus,' Tom said, and groaned and headed out to answer it.

Two weeks ago Tasha would have cut him off but she was learning to back off. She'd learned not to rush to the phone to cut him off from trying to deal with everything himself. In turn, Tom accepted that most calls were Tasha's responsibility. He'd come a long way, she thought. He'd finally accepted that if his body was to heal he had to face its current limitations.

Now he turned to her, his face resigned.

'House call,' he told her. 'Gut pain. I don't know any more. Ron Wetherall. He's a local real estate guru, a big man about town. He's also a bombastic, loud-mouthed bully. He has a mouse of a wife—Iris. Rumour has it that she's his punching bag and I'm sure rumour's right, though I can never get her to admit it. Now he won't tell her exactly what's wrong. Seems he's curled up on the bed, clutching his gut, demanding she ring the doctor. She says he's demanding I be there in two minutes or less—he's in agony.'

Food poisoning? Bowel blockage? Renal colic? There was little to go on, Tasha thought. It could be anything.

'I know he'd rather have me,' Tom told her. 'Macho doesn't even begin to describe our Ron. A woman doctor will just about do his head in. Maybe you could drive me.'

'You're tired,' she said. 'Aren't you?'

And it was a measure of how far they'd come that he agreed. 'Maybe it's time for our macho Ron to accept that women are as skilled as men,' he conceded. 'Are you okay to go?'

'After only one glass of wine?' she said. 'I can do it with my hands behind my back.'

'Then call me if you need me,' he told her, and she smiled at him and he smiled back. She headed out to get her jacket but she had to brush past him as she went.

And she came so close…so incredibly close… to kissing him goodbye that when she reached the veranda it was all she could do not to run.

Iris Wetherall, as Tom had described, was a worried mouse of a woman. She opened the door with a hand to her face, but Tasha could see the beginnings of an ugly bruise under her eye. She ushered Tasha in with relief but Tasha hadn't got two steps inside the door before an agonised moan filled the house. Two small King Charles spaniels put their paws over their heads and moaned in sympathy.

'I don't know what's happening,' Iris whispered. 'I was mopping the kitchen floor. I... Something spilt.' Her hand went to her eye again. 'Ron went to bed and left me to clean but suddenly he started screaming. He's partly undressed, hunched up on the bed, but he won't let me near. He won't say what's wrong, just get the doc, get the doc. He's upstairs.'

Iris hardly had to lead her. All she had to do was follow the moans.

The bedroom was vast. Actually, the whole house was vast, an ode to real-estate luxury surely almost unheard of in modest Cray Point. As she entered the bedroom Tasha had to stop and blink. Acres of white carpet. Vast French windows opening to a massive balcony with spotlights illuminating the swimming pool below. A bed that looked big enough to house a couple of families at a time, and the families wouldn't need to be small. Plush, plush and more plush and in its midst was a florid, overweight man in his fifties, stripped to the waist, his bedcovers half pulled up to hide his nether regions. He was lying almost in a foetal position, moaning fit to die.

'The doctor's here,' Iris quavered, and Ron managed to writhe around so he could see.

'Thank God...'

And then he saw Tasha and his yell almost split the night.

'I said the doc, you stupid cow. I don't want some woman. Get me the doc, now!'

'I'm a doctor.' Tasha was trying to assess what was happening. He was certainly in pain but he was almost apoplectic with rage and his yell had contained strength as well as fury. 'You know Dr Blake's been ill,' Tasha told him. 'I've taken over his house calls. Can you tell me what's wrong?'

'No!' It was a vicious yell, and he turned to his wife again. 'Get her out. I don't want any more stupid women. It's your fault in the first place. Did I ask for new...?' And then he caught himself. 'Get out,' he screamed. 'Now.'

And Tasha was starting to guess what was wrong. If she was right... Ouch.

He did need help. There was no doubting his pain was real, but if he wouldn't let her help…

'I could call an ambulance,' she said.

'I don't want an ambulance. They'll take ages and women work those things now. Get Doc Blake!'

'He isn't on call.'

'Get him,' Ron shouted again.

Tasha hesitated. What she'd like to do was walk away until he saw reason, but there was a chance this was a torsion, something that could mean long-term damage.

'You understand Dr Blake is unwell himself,' she said, playing for time.

'I don't care,' he snarled.

What had Tom's assessment been? *A bombastic, loud-mouthed bully.*

She could call Tom. If she was right in her guessed diagnosis, he might even enjoy it, she conceded, but there was no way she was simply caving to this man's demands. A woman had some pride.

'I could ask Tom to assist,' she said, making herself sound doubtful.

'Get him!'

'Only in an assistant capacity,' she said firmly. 'On that understanding only.'

'He'll do what I tell him.'

'Dear, don't upset the doctor,' Iris quavered, and Tasha gave her a pat on the shoulder.

'I'm not upset,' she told her. 'If Ron doesn't want me to help, then we'll leave him be while we call for back-up.'

'Tom?'

Tom answered on the first ring. He hated Tasha doing these calls without him but he had no choice. The deal was, though, that she call him the moment she was worried.

'Problem?'

'Who would know?' she said softly. 'It might be something serious or it may not. Mr Wetherall is currently clutching his privates, screaming in agony and telling every woman in sight—that's Iris and me—where to go. Iris has the beginnings of a black eye. She looks like she's just been struck. Ron won't say what's wrong but he's demanding that you come. I've finally agreed to call you—but only in an assistant capacity.'

'What do you think's happening?' Ron Wetherall was a beefy oaf, known for his unscrupulous business dealings as well as for his appalling treatment of his rather nice little wife. But if he was really ill...

'He was undressing when it came on,' Tasha said blandly. 'Iris says he had no symptoms until then. He took off his shirt, then his shoes and socks and then started to remove his brand-new pants. That's all the information I've been able to glean. He's told me where to go in no uncertain terms when I asked to examine him, but based on the information...'

And Tom was with her. 'The dreaded zipper stick?'

'That's what I'm assuming. But I'm a girl, what would I know? And it could be something more serious. He's being so obnoxious I could walk out but he could do some real damage.'

'There are those in this town who'd enjoy a bit of real damage,' Tom said thoughtfully. 'But you're right. It'd be negligent to leave him as he is.'

'So you'll come?'

'Of course.' He paused, thinking it through. 'Tasha, I've been worried about Iris for some time. I'm sure she's being assaulted but she won't say. Two months ago I treated her for a broken cheekbone but all she'd say was that she'd fallen. She's had broken bones before but he's always with her when she comes in.'

'She won't talk about her eye now.'

'So we have two patients.' He hesitated and then came to a decision. 'I'm thinking... If he's really incapacitated then maybe we can use this situation to treat the two of them. Will you follow my lead?'

'Of course.'

'Excellent,' Tom told her. 'I'll call the taxi and be right with you.'

Tasha and Iris followed orders and got out of Ron's sight. They drank tea in the kitchen and tried to settle the dogs, while overhead the air was filled with Ron's obscenity-laden moans.

Iris seemed more and more frightened. If this was zipper stick, Ron would need to take his fury out on someone at the end of this, Tasha thought, and she hoped Tom had a plan.

Then Tom arrived—with back-up.

He had a huge surgical case and he had company. Brenda bustled in behind him, carrying surgical scrubs encased in plastic wraps and her own nursing case. She was followed by Karen, the taxi driver, carrying an oxygen canister big enough to fuel an elephant. Tasha tried to take it from her—Tom, plus the district nurse, plus the local taxi driver were all heading for the sick room—but Karen shook her head.

'Doc wants me to carry it,' she said. 'I spend my life hauling luggage. No sweat.'

'Straight up to the bedroom,' Tom ordered. 'I'm not sure what we're facing but Dr Raymond suspects it's serious so we need to get things moving. Dr Raymond, could you come into the bedroom, please? And Iris, too? If this is a surgical procedure we need you to sign consent forms. Karen, could you stay? Karen was a nurse before she and her husband took over the taxi company,' he explained to Tasha. 'We've used her before when we've had to do emergency surgical procedures. She's great.'

And then he reached Ron's bedside and all at once he turned into the Tom Tasha knew. Gentleness itself. 'Hi, Ron. You have a problem? We're here to help and we'll get the pain under control as fast as we can. Let's see what's happening.'

Let's see. Let *us* see. Plural.

There were now five people and two dogs in Ron's bedroom, and Ron was staring wildly up at the assortment of people around his bed. His eyes were almost popping out of his head.

'Get these people out of here!'

'You know I can't do that,' Tom said soothingly. 'I have to assume it's not a minor problem or you would have let Dr Raymond deal with it. And with your request for no ambulance we've come prepared for anything.'

'No,' Ron screamed, and Tom sighed.

'We may need a sedative, Nurse,' he told Brenda. 'Could you administer five milligrams of diazepam, intramuscularly. Karen, would you mind helping? Tasha, I'll get you to hold his hips. Karen, if you could hold that arm? We'll twist him around so he's facing upwards and I can see what we're dealing with. Okay, on my count. Three, two...one...'

And before he knew it, Ron was on his back and Brenda was slipping in the intramuscular sedative.

And they could all see what the problem was.

One penis. One zipper. Inextricably entwined.

Tom grimaced. 'You know, you really should have let Dr Raymond deal with this,' he said gently. 'Swelling around the entrapped tissue makes this procedure more difficult. We need a penile block. Brenda, could you administer...?'

'Certainly, Doctor,' Brenda said.

'You do it,' Ron screamed and Tom shook his head.

'Maybe Dr Raymond could have managed by herself if you'd agreed to let her examine you,' he told him. 'But we've gone past that now. Iris, do you have cooking oil? Excellent. Brenda, can we have a plastic sheet from your bag? Let's move, people. Ron, the sedation will be taking hold any minute. Just try your best to relax until it does.'

Tasha could only watch in admiration. Tom had the situation under complete control.

Once the sedative took hold and they could get a clear idea of how bad the problem was, cooking oil might solve the problem without any other intervention, she thought. The pain was easing but Ron was still breathing fire. He was demanding—expecting—a quick surgical fix, but to his chagrin Tom simply poured cooking oil over everything in sight and told him to stay where he was while the oil had a chance to penetrate.

'It's important you stay still,' he told him. 'The oil may well take half an hour to soften everything around it. Would you like Iris to stay with you? Or Brenda? No? Then I suggest we all re- tire to the kitchen. Call us if there's any change.'

So, much to Ron's fury, they ended up around the kitchen table again. Iris tentatively produced a bottle of wine, which Tom and Tasha refused because they were on duty but which Karen had no qualms in accepting. And Brenda had one too because, as she said, she was only a little bit on duty. Iris watched them drink, and then suddenly poured one for herself.

She drank it too fast, and then Tom poured her another. He was watching her with sympathy. He was waiting, Tasha thought. *What's he doing?*

There was a little small talk. The moans up- stairs were decreasing as the drugs took hold.

Iris was relaxing.

And then, after the second glass of wine, Tom asked Iris about the bruise on her face. She shook her head.

'Tell us,' Tom said gently, and reached over and brushed her cheek, lightly, a gesture of caring that made something inside Tasha twist.

And it must have hit Iris exactly the same way. She gave a half-strangled sob, looked wildly round the table—and then tugged her blouse down to reveal bruises right to where they disappeared under her bra. 'R-Ron,' she said simply. 'All the time.'

'You've never admitted,' Tom said gently. 'Iris, I've asked...'

'He'd hit me harder if he knew I told you. But... but he'll hit me again tonight anyway. He was angry with me before...'

'Do you want to leave him?' Tom asked, and Iris took another gulp of wine and looked wildly about her. Four sympathetic faces looked back.

'Y-yes. But he'd never let me. I don't have any money and I have nowhere to go. He told me once if I ever left him he'd hide everything and he knows how. He says he'll come up on paper as bankrupt. And he'd come after me. No one defies Ron.'

'Iris, we can,' Karen said, in a voice that brooked no opposition. 'And we will. You have two dogs who'd get on fine with my two dogs, who just happen to be German Shepherds. Big ones. My boys are gentle as lambs but they don't look gentle. We have a granny flat at the back of our house and Brian and I and the dogs can see anyone off who needs to be seen off. Promise.'

'And if you don't like the granny flat there's a

spare room at my place,' Brenda told her. 'If you let us…if you allow us to help you, you'll find you're surrounded. Iris, you have friends in this town. Ron's never let them close but we're here for you.'

And suddenly Tasha realised just why Tom had come armed with Karen and Brenda. They'd turned from two nurses into two fierce advocates for a downtrodden sister. Had he known they would? She glanced at him and saw the satisfaction. Of course he'd known.

He cared.

'But then there's money.' Karen sounded not only helpful, she was also practical. 'Ron's loaded but Iris is right—he's smart enough to hide everything. The whole town knows he's a financial snake. I wouldn't mind betting everything's in offshore accounts.'

'Iris, where does he keep his financial records?' Tom's question was gentle but firm. Iris had crossed a line and he didn't want her retreating.

She gazed at him as if he was crazy. As if they were all crazy. But suddenly a flare of hope lit her bruised face. The beginnings of revolt.

'In his study. I'm not allowed in except to dust and hoover.'

'Then let's dust,' Tom said cheerfully. 'And maybe we should dust the insides of his filing cabinet, too. What do you think?'

And, to Tasha's amazement, they were suddenly all in Ron's study. Five people sifting financial documents fast... Operating the copier. Being very, very quiet. At the end of half an hour Iris had a suitcase packed and the dogs and Iris were in Karen's taxi, Brenda following behind to give the impression of solidarity, and Tasha was almost breathless with astonishment.

'We'll get these documents to the local solicitor before his morning coffee,' Tom declared. 'There's no way Ron can hide what he owns now. Iris, you're safe.'

There was still the small matter of one entrapped penis. Ron was still lying rigid in his bed. Tom had warned him not to move and he hadn't.

He looked almost emasculated, Tasha thought, and she could have felt sorry for him if she hadn't seen those bruises. Their staging spoke of constant beatings, over and over.

Tom had taken photographs with his cellphone. 'If it's okay with you, Iris, I'll talk to the police,' he'd said.

And Brenda and Karen had both said, 'Do it.'
Iris had taken another gulp of wine and said
yes.

Ron had quite a day in front of him tomorrow.

But for tonight his pain was almost over. Tasha
was happy to stay in the background. Ron lay
rigid while Tom examined him. The oil had softened the trapped foreskin. The zipper was oiled
to the maximum.

Tom touched the head of the zipper with wire
cutters, the teeth came apart and the skin flopped
free.

There was a tiny bit of bleeding. Tom cleaned
it with care, then he and Tasha removed his oiled
clothing and the plastic sheeting, and helped
Ron into clean pyjamas. Their care couldn't be
faulted.

'We're leaving you another sedative and a couple of painkillers,' Tom told him. 'It's eleven now.
You can take them any time after two. We'll leave
you a glass of water.'

'Iris'll get it,' Ron growled. 'Where is she? I
want a whisky.'

'No alcohol tonight,' Tom decreed. 'Not with
the drugs you have on board.'

'Tell Iris to come up.' And they knew he had no intention of following orders.

'Iris can't come,' Tom said smoothly. 'We noticed bruising on her face and examination proves it's extensive. We've organised for her to stay somewhere where she can be fully examined. Many of those bruises are old. We need to find their cause.'

There was a moment's pause. It stretched.

'She falls,' Ron growled at last. 'Stupid cow. She's clumsy. Don't listen to a word she says. Tell her to come here now.'

'She's already gone,' Tom said gently. 'You get some sleep, Ron. You may need all your strength tomorrow.'

They left him not sleeping. They left him almost rigid with rage and frustration—and fear.

They left and Tom was grinning like the proverbial Cheshire cat.

'I've been waiting for years,' he said in satisfaction. 'I suspected but there was nothing I could do. I can't believe one zipper and it's sorted.'

'She might rescind,' Tasha reminded him. It was sadly normal for battered women to respond to threats and return.

'You think Karen and Brenda will let that happen? They're two of the toughest women I know. Iris has her dogs, a safe place to stay and a couple of German Shepherd watchdogs. She has Karen and Brenda at her back and a file on Ron's dealings that I bet will make our local solicitor's eyes water. Nailed by a zipper.'

'You really do care,' Tasha said slowly. They were back in the car, heading home.

'Do you doubt that? These are my people.'

'Paul never cared.' She hadn't meant to say it. It just…happened.

'I'm not Paul.'

'You surf to the point where you smash yourself on the rocks. You love women.'

'I do,' he said. 'Guilty as charged. So shoot me.'

She fell silent.

So did he.

Guilty as charged.

He accepted it. He knew it.

His care was extraordinary. What had just happened showed a depth of insight and tenderness that almost did her head in. He'd watched and worried about Iris for years, and tonight he'd found an opportunity to put things right.

His care made something inside her twist so

hard it hurt. He loved this town. He loved its people.

So what? The voice inside her head was hammering the question. *It doesn't make any difference. He still loves women. He still loves risk.*

And then the thought of Iris was suddenly front and centre. Once upon a time Iris had loved Ron, she thought. Iris must have gone into marriage as a blissful bride, sure that her man loved her back.

How could you trust your judgement?

She couldn't. Her judgement was skewed by a lousy childhood, but maybe she'd been born with a lack of survival instinct in the first place. Like Iris.

Make decisions with your head, not your heart. She'd said that to herself after Paul's funeral. She'd put the rule aside when she'd tried to have Emily, and hadn't she paid the price?

The night suddenly seemed darker, bleaker, and the exultation from what had just taken place receded. She drove on in silence. Tom stretched his bad leg and winced and she didn't ask about it. She couldn't.

She didn't want to care.

Tom's phone rang and she was almost grateful. He had his phone on speaker and she listened.

Croup. A young mum with an eighteen-month-old baby plus two other children. Her husband was away. She couldn't come to the surgery and Tasha could hear the fear in her voice.

She also heard the unmistakable sounds of croup in the background.

'We're already in the car,' Tom told the young mother. 'We'll be there in less than five minutes.'

'You should be home in bed,' Tasha told him. 'I can do this. Tom, you must be dead on your feet.'

'I have adrenalin bouncing off the walls,' he told her. 'If you think I can go home and sleep...'

'You should do something about your adrenalin. It gets you into all sorts of trouble.'

'Does it?' he asked, and his voice suddenly softened. 'Is that what you're afraid of?'

She didn't answer. She couldn't.

Meg Ainsling was eighteen months old and near to exhaustion. Hannah Ainsling opened the door holding Meg, and she practically fell into their arms with relief.

'I'm so frightened.'

Then she broke off as Meg started wheezing again. It was a fragile, weak cough, a child at the end of her strength.

'You should have rung earlier,' Tom said, swinging his bag onto the table and then taking Meg into his arms.

And here was yet another example of Tom's caring, Tasha thought as he carried the little girl through to the warm kitchen, holding her as if he'd been holding babies all his life. The firmness and his soft growl of reassurance seemed to relax the little one rather than frighten her.

'Let's get some steam into the room,' he ordered. 'Hannah, get every pot you can fit onto the stove, filled with hot water, and see how much we can bring to the boil. Boil the kettle, too. Let's get this room full of vapour.'

That was the old-fashioned way of treating croup, Tasha knew. It worked to an extent but Meg was beyond using that as a sole remedy. Tasha could hear the stridor, which marked the upper airway obstruction secondary to infection or swelling.

She unpacked the medical bag while Hannah started filling the kitchen with steam. Tom performed a swift examination, talking to the little girl as he did. Meg was limp in his arms, as if she sensed that finally here was someone who could help her.

They worked fast, not needing to speak to each other as they worked. There was no need. Tom spooned the little girl back into her mother's arms—after that swift examination there was no need to stress her more than necessary. Then they administered nebulised adrenalin. They used a nebuliser mask with oxygen, and it was a sign of how close Meg was to the edge that the little girl didn't fight it.

Her breathing was rapid. Her pulse was fast and there was a drawing in of the muscles between her ribs and in her neck. It hurt to listen, and Tasha glanced at Hannah's face and glanced away.

She knew this terror. Here it was again, the black wall. The impossibility of moving on.

How could she ever put herself near this dread again? How could she think of having another baby?

How could she let herself love again?

She couldn't.

Hannah had herself under control. 'The stridor will get worse if she cries,' Tom had told her, so every ounce of Hannah's concentration was in keeping her little girl calm.

If it had been Tasha's call she'd probably be

sending her to hospital but Tom seemed content to wait.

Another ten minutes. Another dose.

Tasha accepted his cue. She made them all tea and they waited some more.

Another ten minutes. Another dose.

And finally the stridor faded. The little girl relaxed in her mother's arms, and ten minutes after that she was asleep.

Drama over.

'Keep the steam up tonight,' Tom told her. 'But I think she'll be fine.' They stood by the cot they'd pulled into the kitchen and watched the steady rise and fall of Meg's chest. 'But why did you leave it so long to call?'

'I didn't like to worry you,' Hannah told him. 'I know you need your rest.'

'I'm almost better.'

'But you're not fully better. The whole town knows it. And Tasha—'

'You know Tasha's here to help.'

'But Tasha's little girl would have been the same age as Meg,' Hannah whispered. 'We all know about your Emily, Tasha. We're all so sorry. I didn't want to hurt you.'

And Tasha's chest tightened.

It did hurt. Of course it hurt and it hurt the most because time stood still when it should move on.

Emily was still a part of her, a deep and abiding centre she could never lose. But Emily didn't grow. That was the heartbreak. In her mind Emily was still a beloved, beautiful newborn, not an eighteen-month-old. She should be coping with childhood illnesses, bumps, bruises, all the things that made a normal childhood.

'I don't think about it,' she whispered, and Hannah and Tom looked at her with identical expressions. Expressions that said they knew she was lying.

'I'm not avoiding children for the rest of my life because I've lost Emily,' she said, forcing herself to sound brisk, efficient, professional. 'Are you sure you don't want Meg to go to hospital?'

'She's better with me,' Hannah said, her eyes suddenly welling.

And Tasha thought, *I need to get out of here.*

'Can you take my case out to the car?' Tom asked. 'Sorry, but my leg…'

'Of course.' She knew it was a ruse, an escape Tom sensed she needed, but she was too grateful to protest. 'Goodnight, Hannah. Good luck with Meg.'

'I don't need luck when I have you two,' Hannah whispered. 'God bless both of you.'

Once more she drove. Tom gazed out into the darkness and said nothing. There were things unsaid all over the place.

Hannah's words hung between them.

She wasn't starting any conversation that could end up with her weeping, she decided. She'd spent eighteen months tamping down emotions and she wasn't about to let them flare now.

'How do you cope?' Tom asked, and the tamping got a whole lot harder.

She should say 'I'm fine.' She should say 'It doesn't bother me, seeing kids every day of my working life. Watching parents with kids in strollers, pushing swings in playgrounds, coping with howling kids in supermarkets.'

'I don't cope,' she said quietly. 'I just suck it up and keep it down there. Being a sodden mess for the rest of my life's not an option. Emily's with me as much as she can be. The rest… I think it's like amputation. You learn to get on with your life but nothing's going to put it back.'

He swore.

'And that doesn't help either,' she said. 'You

can't imagine the new words I've attempted.' She tried a smile, which didn't come off. 'I know this is dumb,' she confessed. 'But I used to be afraid of flying. I didn't like thunder either. Now, though, I don't seem to be afraid of anything. It's like the worst has happened, so what can I possibly be afraid of?' She tried for the smile again and finally succeeded. 'So see me indomitable. See me fearless. Just like a Blake boy.'

He didn't smile back. 'I don't like the analogy,' he said softly. 'Because I can't imagine how empty that must feel. If there's anything I can do...' He paused. 'But of course there's not.'

'You did everything you could do.'

'Taking away hurt...'

'It's not possible. It's not worth trying.'

'Tasha, pull in here.' They were driving along the coast road, along the cliffs above the town. There was a track off to the east, innovatively named 'View Road'.

She shouldn't obey, Tasha thought. She was feeling numb, tired by the emotion of the night, exposed by the worry she sensed in Tom's voice. She should keep going, head to bed, hide her pain under her pillows as she fought for sleep.

But the car seemed to turn of its own accord,

and a moment later they were parked under a sign
that was even more innovative—'View Point'.

It was indeed View Point. The moon hung low
over the water, sending silver shards from the horizon straight to Tom's little car. The night was
still and calm. The ocean was a plane of moonlit shimmer.

While they watched, a pod of dolphins broke
the surface just beneath the cliffs. They leaped
in and out of the water as they made their way
south, growing smaller and smaller until all that
was left was a trail of moonlit phosphorescence.

'I ordered those guys,' Tom said smugly. 'Right
on cue. They're good. They'll start demanding a
pay rise soon if they do it any better.'

She'd been lost, caught by the emotion still
welling inside her. Tom's words broke the moment and made her choke on a bubble of laughter.

This was okay. She was moving on.

'What you did tonight was brilliant,' she told
him. 'I can't believe that Iris is safe. And Meg…
How can you care so much?'

'When I'm really like Paul?'

'That's not what I meant.'

'I'm sure it is,' he told her. 'You think I can't
care about anyone because I won't care about

someone in particular. Because I know I'm a risk as husband material, I won't go there, but that doesn't mean I can't care in other ways.'

'I know. I'm sorry.'

'I'm sorry, too. I wish you hadn't had to help treat Meg tonight. I know how much it hurt.'

'I need to get over hurt.' She was trying her hardest to keep this conversation grounded. 'Like you. You're improving every day.'

'I'm not talking about physical hurt. It's the other hurt that stays with us. Watching my father break my mother's heart... Watching your husband betray you... Watching Emily die...' And then he stopped.

There was a long, long silence. She couldn't break it. She didn't know how.

And then...

'Tasha, I'd really like to kiss you.'

This was a bad idea. Her head knew it but somehow tonight she'd passed the point where her head was in control.

The night. The pain she'd just tried to express. His pain.

Tom...

She'd never talked to anyone as she and Tom

had just talked. She'd tried to hide her pain, not put it out there for anyone to see.

Only this wasn't *anyone*.

Tom was her friend. He was the man she'd gone to when she'd been in trouble. He was a colleague, someone who'd helped her, and she could help back. A man who'd suffered a cerebral bleed.

He was all of those things but above all he was Tom.

A man sitting beside her, reaching out to touch her face, swiping away an errant tear that had welled up despite her best efforts to hold it back.

She hadn't cried since she'd left Australia eighteen months before. She'd left her tears in a graveyard high on the headland of Cray Point and she'd shed no tears since.

But somehow Tom exposed her.

She'd just told him she could never feel fear again, and here it was, in the car with them. She was fearful.

Not of Tom. Never of Tom.

She was frightened of how he made her feel.

Turn on the ignition, she told herself. Head for home. Her head was screaming it, but Tom's touch on her face was light, wondering, gentle.

Her friend.

A Blake boy?

The analogy seemed to have gone out the window. She'd watched him comfort a tiny child, calm her, settle her.

She'd watched him care for Iris. Care *about* Iris.

And despite her fears, a flicker of hope lit within her and refused to be quelled.

Maybe she could try... Maybe they could try...

Move forward with your head, not your heart.

Her mantra was wavering. She was trying to clutch at it but it was vaporising at his touch.

'I won't hurt you.' He said it like it was the most sacred vow and somehow she managed to smile.

'By kissing me? You have five o'clock stubble. Of course you'll hurt me.'

'You want to risk it?' The fingers traced her cheekbones, then moved to cup her face, but as if he could sense her fear, his hands held her lightly so she could pull back at any moment.

But fear was receding. Those last tugs from that appalling mantra couldn't hold her. This was Tom.

She raised her face to his and let herself be pulled in to be kissed.

* * *

She hadn't expected it. She hadn't wanted it.
She wanted it now.

His mouth met hers, lightly, tentatively, ready
to pull away if she made the least move of protest.

But how could she protest when it felt as if his
mouth belonged to her? Was part of her. Was...
hers?

For the feel of his mouth on hers wasn't complicated at all. The first touch had deepened in
an instant as both their bodies recognised something bigger than each of them.

Heat. Passion. Desire.

For she wanted him. Her body was screaming
its need and she had no defence. She wanted no
defence. She sank into the kiss and melted into
its heat. She felt his arms wrap around her as if
she was the most precious thing in the world, and
that's what she felt like. Cherished.

Helpless in the face of mutual desire.

Melting and wanting to melt.

But this wasn't exactly a private place. View
Point was also known as Passion Point and for
a reason. The local kids used it as a parking
spot and why wouldn't they? The place breathed
romance.

And now a car zoomed in behind them, all eight cylinders of heated-up metal. It cruised up beside them, the sound system sending out a booming bass that was pretty much guaranteed to break any romantic moment. The driver's window came down and a head poked out.

'Hey, Doc, not expecting to see you up here. You got a chick?'

'That's what I get for not buying a generic sedan,' Tom breathed, and tugged away.

'You too busy to talk?' the kid in the car called, and Tom sighed and wound down his window.

'Time you were home in bed, Benny Lannard,' he said sternly. 'Does your dad know you have his car?'

'Got my licence last week,' Benny said proudly. 'Me and Kylie's just trying things out.'

'Yeah, well don't go trying too much out,' Tom said bluntly. 'You guys know how babies are made and they mean the end of life as you know it. You make Kylie pregnant, mate, you'll be a grandpa at forty and you'll be paying child maintenance for the next twenty years.'

There was a moment's deathly silence.

'Child maintenance...'

'I know you'd do the right thing by Kylie,' Tom

said inexorably. 'But if you don't support her the government garnishes your wages. They take half or sometimes more, until the kid's as old as you are. But of course you know that. And by the way, Kylie, if you end up pregnant you won't get into your nineteen-fifties dresses ever again, and who can go clubbing with a baby in tow? If you think your mum will take over, think again. I know your mum.'

'Uh, gross,' Kylie muttered. 'Benny, maybe...'

'Yeah, babe,' Benny said hurriedly, and Tasha had to choke back laughter at the sudden lack of enthusiasm in both their voices. And then Benny said... 'Who you got there, Doc?'

'A friend,' Tom said, winding his window up firmly. 'A friend who's mature enough to know it's time to go home. We'll leave you to it but if you're planning on starting a family tonight, drop in tomorrow and I'll give you both a brochure on the responsibilities of parenthood.'

They drove home. Tasha was torn between laughter and something else. Something she couldn't name.

The kiss had changed all sorts of things. So had Tom's lecture on responsibility. He cared so much, she thought. He loved this little community and the thought was suddenly, inexplicably sexy.

A doctor giving a lecture on teenage pregnancy? What was sexy about that?

But he'd made her laugh and he'd kissed her again lightly before they'd driven from View Point and every single sense was aware of him. Achingly aware. Nothing else seemed to matter.

Where was sense when she needed it? She couldn't grasp it and she didn't.

And when they reached home the sensation became almost unbearable.

'Cup of tea?' Tom said, and his voice was suddenly unsteady. His voice had been starting to lose the faint slur the stroke had caused and she missed it. Which was dumb. Inexplicable. And then she thought, was she missing it because it meant that soon he'd have no need of her?

Soon she could go home. Wherever home was.

'Or bed?' Tom asked before she could answer the tea question, and the world seemed to still.

Tea and bed. A normal question between friends.

Friends to lovers... It could happen.

It shouldn't happen, she told herself fiercely. It was dumb. She'd fallen for one Blake.

Tom wasn't Paul. He was just... Tom.

And there was no pressure. They ditched their jackets, stowing their medical gear in the hall cupboard. They were two professionals home from the job.

Home. There was that word again.

She was home with Tom.

Home was where the heart was and she knew where her heart lay. Up until now the sense of belonging had seemed everything to do with a tiny grave on a headland but suddenly she knew it wasn't true. Or it was partly true but there was more.

Where was her heart?

It was well and truly here. It was entwined with all the things Tom had done for her. It was entwined with Tom's caring, Tom's laughter, Tom's smile.

Surely not. That'd make a mockery of every vow she'd made after the disaster of her marriage to Paul, but right now her heart didn't seem to connect to her head.

He was so near. So close.

He should have a bigger hallway, she thought tangentially.

And then he said, 'Tasha...' in a voice she hadn't heard before.

A voice full of tenderness. A voice that was husky with a passion that matched what she was feeling.

A voice that said he wanted her as much as she wanted him.

A voice that said bed was inevitable.

'Tom,' she whispered, and the thing was decided. He had her in his arms and he was lifting her...

'Your leg,' she squeaked. 'Your arm...'

'It's therapy,' he told her, smiling. 'You don't think my rehab team would approve of me exercising any way I know how?'

'It's not on your list,' she managed.

'Then it's a dumb list. It needs all sorts of things added to it, starting now.'

CHAPTER EIGHT

SHE WOKE. THE sun was streaming into Tom's bedroom and when she opened her eyes she could see the light glinting on the sapphire surface of the sea. She was in Tom's arms and she'd never felt this way in her life.

She'd thought marriage to Paul had been good. For a short time, before Paul's love of adventure had eclipsed his desire for her, she'd loved their marriage. She'd believed she was loved.

But she'd never felt like this. She lay spooned in Tom's arms and she felt the world settle. This was her place. This was where she was meant to be. Bliss.

But…this was where she'd vowed never to be again.

And bliss or not, her stupid mantra surfaced, uncalled for, unwanted, but it was there all the same. Head, not heart. What had happened last night?

Bliss had happened and it had taken every single piece of sense from her head and dissolved it, until all she'd felt was joy.

And joy was a fleeting, cheating thing. Hadn't she learned that?

But joy was now. She closed her eyes again and pushed away the sense of panic. Surely all that mattered was that she was being held by Tom. This was the man who'd been there for her when she'd needed him most. He'd seen her at her most vulnerable. He'd held her while she'd sobbed and then, as she'd finally tugged herself out of despair, he'd made her laugh again.

He was her lover.

He shouldn't be her lover. That appalling little voice was breaking the moment, ruining the feeling of utter contentment. She lay spooned in Tom's arms, skin against skin, and it felt so right... It felt so wonderful...

Go away, she told her stupid beetle of a mantra, and the mantra backed off a little and tucked itself into a dark corner of her brain.

It was the best she could do. She couldn't wrench it out entirely.

But she wanted to give herself up entirely to this man. She wanted to think happy ever after. She wanted the whole fantasy.

But the beetle was still asking questions. How many women had he had in this bed? How many more would share it in the future?

She stirred and his hold on her tightened, strong, warm, possessive. 'Good morning, my love,' he whispered, his voice muffled by her hair, and she felt like screaming at her beetle. Go away, go away, go away.

She'd gone this far. Why not embrace this moment? She turned within his arms and felt herself melt again. She was where she wanted to be more than anything else in the world.

She was home.

I don't think so, the beetle told her, and she knew it spoke the truth. But for now... Please let me believe it as truth.

And she did. Sort of. Her body turned to his again and it felt right. It felt perfect.

She was so in love.

She was so in trouble.

Tasha was different.

He'd never felt this way with a woman before.

She was his friend. He felt as if he'd known her forever. He felt as if he knew her through and

through, and making love with her had been inevitable.

He loved her.

Until last night he would have said he loved
her as a friend, nothing more. Or maybe he was
lying. Maybe he'd wanted her for a very long
time but he hadn't acknowledged it until now.

But there was no choice but to acknowledge it
now. The way he felt...

Was it possible that he could trust himself to
commit?

Was it possible that Tasha was the one?

And there it was, a thunderbolt of knowledge
so deep it almost knocked him sideways. He'd
never thought he could be faithful to a woman,
but he'd never met Tasha.

With Tasha all bets were off. Family history be
damned. He could be faithful. He would be faithful and suddenly, fiercely, he knew it at a level
so deep that the years of doubt fell away.

He'd teach her to trust, he thought. If he could
learn the lesson then so could she.

But for now... Enough of the introspection, he
told himself as he gathered her against him yet
again. He had this woman in his arms and that
was all that mattered.

He asked for nothing more in the world.
But then the world broke in.

Susie...
Theirs had been a fleeting relationship, not
even consummated. She'd been fun. She'd now
found a man she wanted a permanent relationship with, and that was fine by him. They were
still friends.

But why was she on his veranda at this hour?
'Tom. Yoo-hoo... Tom, love, are you awake?
It's Susie. Sorry, sweetheart, I understand you
should be resting but you know I left my shawl
here? Donald's taking me away for the weekend
and I need it.'

If there was anything surer to bring Tasha's mantra beetle out of its dark corner, this was it.

Susie. A woman from Tom's past.

Only how did she know she was from his past?

Because he'd told her? Because she trusted
Tom?

Maybe she did—but, oh, the level of faith she
had to have...

She didn't have enough.

Tom hauled on a pair of pants while Tasha lay

back and cringed and the gorgeous feeling of being cherished turned to smut.

He opened his wardrobe and grabbed a shawl, which made her feel even worse.

This was innocent, she told herself. This was Tom's past life and it had nothing to do with her, but head was suddenly ruling heart in no uncertain terms. It was fear. It wasn't logical but she was a coward, and she knew it.

Tom had walked out onto the veranda. He was speaking briefly to Susie, but she wasn't listening. Fear had her hauling on knickers, bra, jeans and windcheater, and by the time he came back to the bedroom she was dressed.

'Tasha...' He came straight to her. He must be able to see the fear on her face. She couldn't disguise it from herself, much less him. 'Love, it's not what it seems. Susie left her shawl here months ago, before the accident. Hilda must have packed it into the wardrobe. I saw it when I came home from hospital but I didn't have the energy to do anything about it. She asked me about it last week. I told her where it was but then I forgot again. Then...to be honest...Tasha, I haven't been thinking of Susie. You've been here...'

'Your latest conquest,' she muttered. 'How can I have been so dumb?'

'Tasha...'

'Leave it, Tom,' she said roughly. She felt sick. Betrayed.

Not betrayed by Tom, though. He'd broken no promises. She was even sure that he was speaking the truth.

The betrayal she felt was worse. She'd betrayed herself, her own beliefs, her own hard-earned self.

'I never slept with Susie,' he said flatly.

'Tom, I believe you. I'm sorry. The conquest jibe was unfair. I do know you better than that. But you're my friend, Tom, not my lover, and risking that by fancying myself in love with you is just plain dumb. It scares me. It makes me feel out of control and I've vowed never to go down that path again.'

And then she took a deep breath and said what had to be said. What her mantra dictated she had to say.

'Tom, I'll be grateful for you forever. Please, if possible I'll always be your friend, but because there's this attraction between us then the friendship has to be at a distance. We both know that.

So I'll stay in Cray Point until you can drive again. I'll stay until you don't need to do rehab every day, but I won't stay here.'

'That's crazy.'

'Cats make me sneeze,' she said, striving desperately for lightness, and then she decided to say it like it was. 'But they don't break my heart, and if I stay here that's what I'm risking. I never meant you to be my lover and I don't want that.'

'I didn't think I wanted it either.' His voice was serious, troubled, and she saw real concern for her in his gaze. It was almost her undoing.

But the feeling she'd had as he'd tugged Susie's shawl from the wardrobe was one she'd never wanted to feel again. Okay, she believed him. Susie was simply an ex who'd left her shawl here, but it had opened a chasm in her heart that had been ripped open the moment she'd heard Paul on the phone to the other woman.

She hadn't wanted to believe it. She'd asked Paul calmly who he'd been on the phone to. Honesty in marriage, she'd thought, and she'd expected a confession.

And then he'd lied, and she'd known he'd lied. She knew Tom was speaking the truth now, but lies or truth, that chasm was still there. To trust herself...

No. She was self-contained. What had started with Paul had torn her heart. She'd got over his deceit and his death—sort of—and then she'd thrown her hat into the ring again in the loving business and she'd tried to have a baby. And that had ripped her heart almost out of her body.

What was she doing, thinking she could start again?

She couldn't.

She had an appointment with the IVF clinic in six weeks. The prospect had been so huge it had terrified her, but the seed of hope had flared and grown.

And now...one night of passion and one stupid shawl had shown her how stupid that hope was. She couldn't be brave. She'd had the brave crushed out of her.

She had no courage left.

'Tasha, you look terrified.' Tom was watching her, worried for her, reaching for her, but she backed away.

'I'm not. At least, I'm not as long as I can get away. Tom, you've been the best friend but now... I don't want this to go further and in your heart

I don't think you do either. I'm sorry, Tom, but it's you or the cats, and it's time I was sensible. I choose cats.'

'I'm scared, too,' he said, almost as if he hadn't heard her, and she blinked.

'I said I wasn't.'

'I know you are. Like me. We're peas in a pod. Tasha, I've spent my life thinking guys who married and remained faithful for the rest of their lives had some sort of gene that was missing in my family.' He took a deep breath. 'It turns out I was wrong. It turns out it was just that I hadn't met the right woman.'

It should have made her melt, but how could she? She was holding herself rigidly under control, clinging to the knowledge of past hurt. 'I'm not that woman,' she managed.

'You've been burned. First by my idiot half-brother. Second by the loss of Emily, though the loss of your parents has to be in the mix there as well. You don't trust love, just as I didn't. But it's past tense, Tasha. I trust it now. You can choose to trust me or not...'

'How can I do that?'

Silence. The room was deathly still. It was as

if the weight of the world was right above their heads, ready to descend.

Tasha was feeling ill.

Trust. Her heart was crying for it, longing for it, aching for it as if there was a void in there that only trust could fill.

She could take this one step…

And fall into the arms of Tom Blake. And try for another baby.

And let the whole disastrous cycle start again.

And her heart clenched. She could almost feel it shrivel at the thought of what could lie ahead if she fell into the arms of this man.

She'd hurt so much…

Cats.

'I'm… I'm leaving,' she whispered. 'Please, Tom, don't try and stop me. If you keep pressuring I won't be able to stay at Hilda and Rhonda's. I'll have to go away completely.'

'Are you so afraid?'

And finally she gave him the truth. 'Yes,' she said, openly and honestly. 'Yes, I am.'

'You can't take a chance on me?'

'I can't take any more chances. I'm being sensible.'

'So sensible means we stay alone for ever?'

'I know how much it hurts...'

'So you'll teach me?' Anger was obvious now, raw and exposed. 'I've finally met the woman I want to spend the rest of my life with, but she's scared I might betray her.'

'Tom...'

'I wouldn't,' he said fiercely. 'I won't. But of course you're right, I have no evidence to back that with. You've judged me on my father and on Paul...'

'I'm not...'

'There's no need to go on,' he snapped. 'You've said enough. I care about you, Tasha, but I have nothing more than my word to prove it. So I can't prove it. We'll leave it there, then. We'll work out the nuts and bolts of how we plan the workload later. You've made your choice. Go and live with cats.'

CHAPTER NINE

'I THINK WE can safely say you're all right to drive again.'

Of all the things he'd been hoping for, this should have been the biggest. Sally had just performed intensive neurological tests. She'd pushed him every way she could. His left leg was still weaker than the right. He still had a slight limp. His fingers didn't flex instantaneously but they were pretty fast. In these last four weeks he'd pushed himself to the physical edge and now he was reaping the rewards.

He was cured. Well, almost. Recovery from cerebral damage was slow. His brain was making new neural pathways. He still had a way to go before he could balance well on a surfboard again, but essentially his body could almost be classified as normal.

He should be over the moon.

He walked out of the physiotherapy clinic and missed Tasha.

She still came with him occasionally, but she'd ceased joining in. She sat on the sidelines, silently, reading a book, pretending she wasn't watching. Anger still vibrated between them. It felt as if they'd betrayed each other. A normal friendship was impossible.

She hadn't come today. Darryl and Louise Coad had turned up at the surgery to discuss their worries about their elderly mother. Tasha could have put them off until tomorrow, or she could have asked Tom to see them later—they were, after all, his patients—but instead she'd welcomed them.

'Of course I can see you. Tom, can you ask Karen to drive you?'

She'd sounded almost relieved, which was the story of their lives right now. She didn't want anything more to do with him than she had to.

Her fear left him feeling angry. Why couldn't she trust when he'd made such a leap himself?

'Why the black face?' He'd been sitting in Karen's cab, silent, his thoughts grim as Cray Point's taxi driver took him home. 'I would have thought you'd be on top of the world,' she said. 'Great report from your physio. And, hey, did you know the solicitors have put a freeze on Ron's assets?

Iris should be set for life. There's also a question about the legality of Ron's financial dealings. Some of those documents we copied are red hot. The local cop says we might end up with Ron facing charges other than assault and battery. How cool's that?'

'Really cool,' Tom said, and tried a smile, but Karen looked sideways at him and grimaced.

'You got it bad, huh?'

'What?'

'Don't *what* me. The whole town knows you're loopy over Tasha. We all know why she moved out and we're all really sorry. And now you've recovered, she can leave and we'll be stuck with your sorry face for the rest of our lives. Whatcha going to do about it, Doc?'

'There's nothing I can do,' he said explosively. 'She loved my half-brother and he was a toe rag. She lost her baby. How do I persuade her to trust again?'

And there it was, out in the open. He'd said it. He sat back, aghast, feeling more exposed than he'd ever felt in his life.

Karen didn't say anything. There was nothing to say, at least for the moment. It took her a good two minutes before she opened her mouth again and even then it wasn't to impart wisdom.

'Guess flowers and candles and Hilda's casseroles won't work on this one, hey, Doc?'

He almost lost it. He gritted his teeth and they drove on in silence.

When finally they pulled up outside the surgery he had himself under control—almost. 'Thank you,' he said curtly. 'Put it on my account.'

'Sure thing, Doc.'

'And don't go saying—'

'I don't need to. The whole town knows. Tasha's looking as grim-faced as you. I don't know why we don't just knock your heads together and be done with it.'

'And put us both back into hospital with cerebral bleeds?'

'Not funny, Doc,' she said. She paused. 'You know Rhonda and Hilda and their dad will be back on Sunday. If you've got your driving licence back and they're wanting their house, what's to stop Tasha from leaving?'

'Nothing.' Except a small grave up on the hill, but that wouldn't hold her, he thought.

And he couldn't hold her.

'Think of something, Doc,' Karen said urgently. 'There must be some way…'

'Leave it, Karen,' he said heavily, and slammed the taxi door and headed up to the house.

He limped. When he concentrated he no longer limped but he wasn't concentrating on his leg now.

He was thinking of nothing but Tasha.

The post box was full. He grabbed it as he went past, and riffled through. He wanted something—anything—to distract him, but there seemed nothing out of the ordinary. They all looked like specialist letters sent after referrals, all like the dozen or more he sorted at the end of each day.

He poured himself a beer and settled down to read. Work… It was the only way he could think of to get his head away from where it most wanted to be.

Rhonda and Hilda shared a picturesque cottage in the centre of town. It was cute to the point of twee, filled with mementos of lives back in England, husbands now gone, shells collected over years, pieces of driftwood, china ornaments, cats past and present.

Tasha was currently sitting on the back step overlooking a hundred or so pot plants. Cats were twining through her legs and her eyes were watering.

She wasn't noticing. She was staring in horror at a small white stick.

A stick with two red lines in the centre.

How had this happened? *How?*

She'd been a bit queasy yesterday and the day before. And tired. Then she'd woken in the middle of the night thinking dates. Thinking horror.

This morning she'd lost her breakfast.

She tested herself at the surgery and told herself it must be a mistake. She'd pleaded that it was a mistake. Then she'd worked all day, thrusting it on the backburner.

She'd just tested herself again.

If she was asked to describe her feelings right now, she couldn't. Of all the dumb, terrifying, catasmotic—was that a word?—things to happen…

She was pregnant with Tom's child.

One night.

They'd used condoms. Of course they had—they weren't kids like Benny and Kylie. They'd stopped before things had got out of hand. They'd decided—like mature adults—to go ahead but to be careful.

She'd been sensible. Tom had been sensible.

Okay, they might have been in a hurry...

This was too big. Her head couldn't take it in. She was staring at the red lines until they blurred.

She was exposed again. She was totally, absolutely out of control, when she'd made a conscious, intelligent decision to stay in control. She'd moved out of Tom's house four weeks ago and she'd kept her distance. Even if her heart did give this crazy hammer every time she saw him, she had it under wraps. She was being sensible.

Rhonda was due home tomorrow and Hilda and their dad soon after. She'd intended to stay on in their guest room, work here for a couple more weeks until she was sure Tom could cope, and then go... Where?

It didn't matter. She'd intended to start looking at job offers soon. Somewhere busy, she'd thought. Somewhere demanding where her head didn't have to think.

Of Emily. Or Paul. Or her parents.

Or betrayal and loss.

Or Tom.

She'd written to the IVF clinic and asked them

to destroy the last vials of Paul's sperm. She had no use for it. She knew she didn't have the courage to start again.

The plastic stick in her hand with its red lines made a mockery of every single decision she'd made.

She felt dizzy and more than a little sick. Her hands went instinctively to her belly.

A foetus.

A baby.

'Tasha?'

Of all the people she most didn't want to face right now it was Tom. She gasped as she saw him appear at the back gate. Her hand instinctively dropped and she let the small white stick fall through the planks between the steps.

Somehow she forced a smile.

He was wearing his customary jeans and ancient T-shirt. He was smiling at her just the way she loved him to smile.

Tom.

The father of her baby.

She thought she might faint.

'Are you okay?' He knew her well, this man. He opened the gate and came towards her, looking worried, and she made a huge effort and summoned a smile to greet him.

'H-hi. Yes, I'm fine.' And then she thought he wouldn't believe that. She knew she'd lost colour. 'I think I ate something at lunch,' she told him. 'I did a house call on Bert Hathaway and he insisted I try one of his homemade sausages. It's been sitting like a lump of lead in my stomach all afternoon.'

'He makes great sausages.'

'Says the man with a cast-iron stomach. Do you know how much chilli he puts in those things?'

'That's why I know they're safe. No bug could stand the heat. Are you vomiting? Need a nice injection? I'm just the man for the job.'

'I'm sure you are but no, thanks.'

'And I have the all-clear to give as many injections as I want,' he told her, smiling down at her. 'As of today I have my driving licence back. I'm classified normal.'

That was good—wasn't it? She was so confused her head was having trouble operating her tongue. 'Your arm and leg still aren't what they should be,' she managed.

'I'll keep on with the rehab,' he told her. 'But I'm improving every day. Thanks to you.'

'Just because I'm bossy...'

'Sometimes a man needs bossy,' he said, and sat down on the step beside her.

She didn't want him to sit down. She wanted to get up and run.

The sun was almost down. The sky was tinged with the gold of a truly amazing sunset. Grass parrots were settling in the gumtrees around the house, squawking as they fought for the best nesting perch. A cat was purring across her feet. Two more were prowling under the steps.

She was sitting on the back step with the man she loved with all her heart, and all she wanted to do was run.

'Tasha,' he said gently, and her heart did a back flip.

'I... Yes.'

'A letter came to the surgery today,' he told her. 'It was addressed to Dr T. S. Blake. I'm T. R., but I didn't notice. It was in a pile of specialist letters. They all look the same and I didn't even think. I opened it and read it before I realised. I'm sorry.'

And he flipped a letter from his back pocket, tugged it open and handed it over.

It was a formal letter from the IVF clinic.

Dear Dr Blake

We have received your letter advising us that you wish us to cancel your appointment and dispose of the sperm held in your name. To do this, however, we need you to complete the attached legal documents.

You are required to have the forms witnessed...

Please return the forms to...

Documents were attached. This was the formal acknowledgement that she wished never to have a child.

That she wished for no more pain.

She held the letter in her hand and watched the letters blur, as the lines on the pregnancy test had blurred moments ago. Her head felt like it might explode. She wanted to shrink into nothing. Disappear.

'I guess Paul used your married name when he deposited the sperm,' Tom said helpfully from the sidelines. 'Though I would have thought they'd use your full name.'

'I'm sorry,' she said, because she couldn't think what else to say.

'You don't need to apologise.' He put a hand

over hers. 'Tasha, was this decision because of us? Were you intending to try for another child and cancelled because of what happened between us?'

'It's nothing to do with you.' Except it was. Now it was.

'I can't bear it,' he said at last. 'That I hurt you...'

'You didn't hurt me.'

'I know I wasn't meant to read it,' he said. 'But this letter tells me you'd made the decision to try again for a baby, and now you've cancelled.' He shook his head. 'Tasha, they attached a copy of your letter. You wrote it the day you moved out of my home.'

'I should be grateful,' she whispered. 'I'd forgotten how much love hurts. All you did was remind me. This decision is all about me, not about you.'

'Tasha...'

And then he paused, his attention caught by what was happening at his feet.

Two cats had been snooping under the steps where they'd been sitting. They were agile, curious Burmese, ready to play with anything.

Neither Tasha nor Tom had been paying them

attention but they'd been playing with something. Batting it forward.

Now one creamy paw batted their plaything out from the narrow opening under the bottom step. The cats had to go sideways to get out, so for a moment their toy lay untended.

It was a white plastic stick. It showed two red lines facing upwards.

Tasha couldn't move. She sat frozen as Tom reached forward, almost idly, as if it was of no importance at all that he was picking up a pregnancy test stick and reading the results.

The cats yowled their protest that their toy had been taken from them. The parrots kept on squawking overhead. The surf was a faint hush-hush in the background.

All Tasha heard was white noise. The world spun. And then Tom was pushing her head down between her knees, holding her, supporting her while she decided whether to retch or faint—or do nothing.

Nothing was safest. Nothing was what she wanted most in the world.

Tom sat silent and let her have her nothing.

It couldn't last. Of course it couldn't. She sat, head bowed, while Tom ran his fingers through her curls and the silence between them built to a crescendo.

When Tom finally spoke his voice sounded as if it came from a long way away. 'Tasha...' He stopped, cleared his throat and tried again. 'Tasha, are you pregnant?'

'I... Yes.' There was nothing else to say.

He looked at the stick again, then set it aside to pick up the letter and re-read. 'This means... Tasha, did you contact the IVF people to cancel *before* you knew you were pregnant?'

'Yes.' What did he think? That she'd deliberately used his sperm instead? The thought made her want to laugh but there was no way she could laugh. She was so close to hysterics.

Unbidden, her hands went to her belly again. Tom noticed. She knew he'd noticed.

He started stroking her hair again, as one would stroke a wounded wild creature, giving reassurance that help was at hand. Only help wasn't at hand. She was flailing. 'We were careful,' he said, and she heard shock underneath the caring.

She had to make herself talk.

'One of my professors once said the only sure contraceptive is a brick wall,' she managed. 'Tom, I'm sorry.'

Her voice was muffled. She had to straighten. She did but heaven only knew the effort it cost her. To sit up and face the world...

To sit up and face Tom.

'When did you find out?' he asked, still in that strange, neutral voice.

'I've been off colour for a couple of days. This morning...' She bit her lip. 'I woke up and knew. I just knew.'

'So just today.'

'Y-yes.'

'And it's mine.'

That was harder. She had to struggle to make her lips move. 'Yes.' She should say something else, she thought, but she couldn't make herself think what.

Would he be angry?

He didn't sound angry.

Of all the sensations whirling around them right now, anger didn't seem one of them.

There was a long silence. It must have hit him like a sledgehammer, she thought, but the sledgehammer had been at work on her as well and she didn't have a clue where to take this. But finally he spoke.

'Tasha, could you bear to have it?'

And there it was, out in the open.

Could she have Tom's baby?

The thought was so immense it took her breath away. To carry a baby for nine months? To give birth to a little one who looked like Tom? To watch Tom fall in love with his child as she knew instinctively that he would?

Family. The chasm was right before her but instead of running away she seemed to have stepped forward so one foot was in mid-air. Maybe both feet were.

'Tasha, don't look like that.' He turned her face with his lovely strong hands, forcing her to meet his gaze. 'Love, this little one's safe. You know the odds of what happened to Emily are so small that they melt into insignificance. There's nothing to say our baby won't be perfect.'

There it was. *Our baby.* She was trapped in her own terror. Her hands still clutched her belly.

Tom's hand closed over hers and held.

'Tasha,' he said, strongly, forcefully. 'This will be okay. This will be good. We can do this.'

We. There it was again.

'Tasha, you can trust me.'

At least he got it, she thought. At least he understood the chasm of faith that was required—faith that she was unable to give.

But she couldn't answer him. She tried but no words came out.

'Cup of tea,' he said, suddenly cheerful. He schecked out the stick's red lines again, then tucked it into his pocket. 'Yep, I'd call that a definite positive. We should keep this. It's the first entry in our baby's memento book. But meanwhile, tea with lots of sugar. I could handle a beer but just this once I'll forgo it. Two mugs of tea coming up.'

Tasha stayed on the step, gazing at nothing. Tom headed into the kitchen, found the mugs among the kitsch and made two mugs of tea.

And tried to come to terms with what he'd just learned.

Tasha was having a baby.

His baby.

Their baby.

The thought was almost overwhelming.

He'd never imagined this. As long as he could remember, he'd thought of himself as a loner. Relationships couldn't be trusted. He couldn't be trusted. He'd never met a woman who he'd known he could commit to for the rest of his life and he'd assumed he never could.

And then there was Tasha. For the first time he'd felt the beginnings of trust in himself. For the first time he'd thought that here was a woman he wanted to spend the rest of his life with. Betrayal was out of the question because this was Tasha. Hurting Tasha, betraying Tasha's trust, would be like ripping out a part of himself.

He suddenly found himself thinking of that tiny grave high on the headland. Of Emily. Of the way her tiny fingers had curled around his. Of the way her wide eyes had struggled to focus. Of the feel of her tiny body against his. Her newborn smell.

He wanted it. He ached for it.

He wanted a family.

How far had he come since he'd met Tasha?

And how to ease her pain now?

He took the tea outside and she was still staring sightlessly down at Rhonda's pot plants. He stared for them for a while, too. They were pretty boring.

'Seen one geranium, seen 'em all,' he ventured, and Tasha hiccupped on something that might have been a sob. He sat down and pressed her tea into her hands.

'Drink.'

'I don't need—'

'Doctor's orders. Drink.'

She did. Slowly. He drank his, too, and by the time they'd finished the sun had set and it was almost dark.

'I don't know what to do,' she whispered at last.

He took her empty mug and set it down on the veranda and tried to find a way in.

'Do you want a termination?' The words were a slash across the silence of the night and she drew in her breath with a shocked hiss.

But she didn't answer straight away. It's on the table, he thought, and the sensation hurt.

The silence stretched on. Finally her hands went back her belly, the movement a protective gesture as old as time itself.

'No,' she whispered. 'How can I? It's real. A baby…'

'Our baby,' he said again into the night, feeling almost light-headed with relief. He'd never thought he wanted a child. Why was he suddenly desperate for this one? His hands rested against hers as he searched for the next thing to say. The right thing. 'Tasha, whatever else is between us, this is non-negotiable. You're not doing this as a single parent. I'm with you every step of the way. I know you don't trust me. I know you don't want a relationship between us and I accept that. But you will need support...'

'So here it comes again,' she managed, suddenly sounding dreary. 'You support me during Emily's loss. I support you after your injury. You support me while this one's born... We're taking turns.'

'It doesn't need to be taking turns,' he said softly. 'We can support each other forever.'

'Tom...'

'I know—you can't,' he said. 'So we'll do what we need to do to care for this little one with all the love we can muster.'

'I don't want to stay here.' It was a wail and he gave a rueful smile.

'There's no need for you to stay.'

'But it's your baby.'

'And if I need to, I'll leave Cray Point.'

She turned and stared at him in stupefaction. 'You'd leave...'

'I've hardly thought this through,' he said ruefully. 'But my initial feeling... Tasha, if you need to return to England, then maybe I can, too. Don't worry. I won't turn into some weird stalker. We can still live separate lives but I'll not ask you to parent on your own. I can get work wherever.'

'But you love it here.'

'I love you.'

The words seemed to take all the air from her lungs. She was flailing. 'Tom...'

'I never thought I'd say those words but it's true,' he continued. 'You don't want it and I accept that, but, Tasha, I will love our baby. I'll be there whenever you need me and whenever he or she...' He frowned. 'Who is this, by the way.'

'I have no idea,' she snapped, torn between tears and laughter. 'The pregnancy test doesn't come with blue for boy, pink for girl. It's currently the size of a tadpole.'

He grinned, that gorgeous smile that had her heart twisting. 'I wasn't talking about our baby's gender. I was talking of names. Hey, my grandma used to call tadpoles pollywiggles. How's that for a name? Yes? Okay, I'll be there whenever Pollywig needs me. Birth? If you want me there, check. Teething? I sing a cool lullaby as long as she's into Pink Floyd. First day at school? I'll probably cry.'

'Tom!' She was practically crying herself. 'You can't put your life on hold...'

'See, that's what I hadn't figured,' he said gravely, and his hands tightened on hers. 'But finally I have it sorted. Life isn't Cray Point. Life is family.'

'Tom, I can't…' It was practically a wail.

'You don't need to do anything,' he told her. 'You definitely don't need to commit to me. All I ask is that you accept you have family. I'm your ex-half-brother-in-law who's now the father of your baby. That seems pretty much family to me.' And before she knew what he was about he leaned forward and kissed her lightly on the lips. It was a feather kiss, a fleeting touch, a gesture of reassurance and warmth. Surely nothing more.

'Are you sure you don't need anything for nausea?' he asked. 'I'm starting to not believe your sausage story.'

'It was a fib,' she confessed.

'So…morning sickness?'

'Nothing I can't handle.'

'Tasha, you will ask for help?'

She took a deep breath. 'I will ask for help.'

'And you'll stay for the next two weeks at least.'

'I will do that.' Because what option did she have?

But suddenly she thought, *The terror has faded.*

The overwhelming, paralysing fear when she'd seen those two lines had dissipated.

'Pollywig...' she said tentatively, and he smiled and touched her hair.

'It's a fine name, but we can discuss options if you like.'

'I like Pollywig.'

'So do I.' He rose and smiled down at her. 'And I like Pollywig's mum. But Pollywig's mum needs to head to bed and get her head around the new norm. And me... I'm heading out behind the wheel of my little car to celebrate the fact that I can drive again. And I'm going to be a dad. It's been quite a day.'

'It has. Tom...'

'Mmm?'

'Thank you.'

'Think nothing of it,' he said grandly. 'And don't you dare go to bed and tremble. Together we can cope with one cute Pollywig. Together we can do anything.'

And he leant forward again and his lips brushed her forehead.

And then he was gone and the night was darker for his going.

* * *

Who could sleep?

She lay in bed and stared up at the darkness and called herself all kinds of coward.

Tom loved her. She knew it. She could see it in the way he looked at her. She could feel it in the way he touched her. She just...knew it.

It would be so easy to walk into his arms and let the future take over.

Become Mrs Blake again? Pregnant.

Rhonda and Hilda had left strict instructions as to the temperature the cats needed for comfort. The house was constantly overheated, but right now she was cold.

Why was she shaking? It wasn't as if she was frightened of Tom, and surely logic would decree that this pregnancy should be fine. The odds were on her side.

She was pregnant with Tom's baby. She suddenly felt a burst of warmth amid the fear.

This baby would be Tom's. He wanted to be its father.

Pollywig.

'It's a lousy name for a baby,' she said out loud, and she almost found the courage to smile.

Tom had said he'd move from Cray Point to be a father. She couldn't make him do that.

So live here? He'd suggested a medical partnership.

But part of her shut down at the thought. Working with Tom every day... She couldn't.

Why? she asked herself, but the same part refused to answer.

Because she loved Tom? Because she couldn't bear to see him every day?

Because she was a coward?

None of those things, she told herself savagely. It was just that there was an attraction between them that couldn't be denied, and she was being sensible. She wanted no part of it so she needed to leave.

But she couldn't go back to England. It wouldn't be fair to Tom.

Or to her?

For home felt like here.

'It does not.' She said it out loud and one of the cats wandering past her bedroom door leaped in fright and bolted for the company of his mates. 'I don't have a home.'

'You'll need to make one. So think about sensible.'

Sensible was what she needed. She needed to make plans, get herself under control again, stop the crazy vortex in her head once and for all.

'Summer Bay.' There was a sensible thought. Summer Bay, where Tom had gone to rehab, was a town big enough for a large medical centre with half a dozen doctors. She could get a job, relieving at first, and then as Pollywig grew maybe full-time work.

She had money from Paul's life insurance. She could buy a wee house.

Maybe a puppy...

Tom could visit. The towns were only half an hour apart. It was a sensible distance, where Tom could be as involved as he wanted with Pollywig but their lives could be as separate as they needed to be.

'I wouldn't even have to know who he was dating.' She said that out loud, too. It should have sounded sensible. It should have sounded reassuring but instead it came out a bit...petty?

All of a sudden she felt silly and just a little bit small. To not have the courage to trust...

'I can't help it,' she told the night, and the night just had to listen. 'I'm not built to trust again.'

'You're a coward.'

'Yes, but I'm a pregnant coward and I need to look after me for my baby's sake.'

'That's an excuse and you know it.'

'Okay, I'm afraid,' she said out loud. 'I'm a great blob of yellow custard, quivering at the edges, and there's not a thing I can do about it. So go to sleep.'

She closed her eyes but sleep wouldn't come. The quivering wasn't helping.

CHAPTER TEN

RHONDA RETURNED THE next day. Hilda was arriving later, with their father. 'There's been a hitch in his visa arrangements but he should be here in two weeks,' Rhonda told Tasha, and Tasha thought that was excellent. That'd give her two weeks to finalise things here and find somewhere to live in Summer Bay.

'How's Tom?' Rhonda asked, and Tasha thought of all the things she could say—but didn't.

'His recovery's remarkable,' she said instead. 'He still has left-sided weakness but it's fading almost to unnoticeable. Another month and he should be back to normal.'

'But you're only staying for two more weeks?' Rhonda looked at her sharply. 'And you've moved in here. Conflict? Tom's women?'

'He's not dating at the moment but that's part of it,' she agreed. 'I didn't want to get in the way of his lifestyle.'

'You do know he doesn't enjoy his lifestyle

very much,' Rhonda told her. Rhonda's luggage was still in the hall and the cats were tangling themselves round her legs in ecstasy, but she was homing right in on Tom as if she'd been worrying the entire time she'd been away. She probably had.

'There are lots of good women in Cray Point,' Rhonda told her. 'Our Dr Tom is quite a catch. He's always been a looker, and he's lovely. Clever and skilled and kind. But even when he was a teen he dated girls who were older, more experienced, less likely to be clingy. His mother used to worry. Why didn't he find himself a nice girl who wanted to settle down and have babies? We could see it, though. His mother was a watering pot. She never disguised the fact that Tom's father broke her heart, and she never let Tom forget the fact that he looked just like his father.

'"Don't you ever do that to a girl," she'd say over and over, and she'd say it to everyone. "I do hope he doesn't turn out like his dad." She was a beautiful ninnyhammer, our Marjorie, and I reckon it's affected Tom all his life. If you say something to a child often enough, he'll believe it. At least no one's saying it to him now but it's probably too late. How can we get our Dr Tom to commit?'

She already had, Tasha thought bleakly. He had committed.

But she'd done just what his mother had done.

She'd accused him of being like his father. And his brother.

Worse, she'd believed it. A part of her still did believe it and she wasn't brave enough to walk away from that belief.

For the next few days things seemed to slow down. Life felt in slow motion. It was a strange sensation but that was how she felt. She had slight morning sickness but not much. She kept waiting for the signs of miscarriage but none came. She kept feeling the pregnancy was some sort of dream, but a week later, when she went to see the charge doctor of the Summer Bay medical group about a job, she confessed that her work would be part-time. And because Adam Myers' specialty was obstetrics, she confessed why and ended up having a full examination.

'Lovely and normal,' Adam told her, and when she told him what she was most afraid of, he pulled the stats up on the internet and told her what the chances were of it happening again.

'Somewhere between infinitesimal and none,' he told her. 'We'll scan at twenty weeks. A good paediatric cardiologist should pick up on any problems then, but I'm willing to bet my new employee's monthly wage cheque on a good out-come.' His kindly face creased into a smile of concern. 'It'll be great to have you on board, Tasha. Having a new emergency physician will be amazing. But tell me...' He hesitated. 'Why are you leaving Cray Point? I hear Tom Blake's desperate for a partner.'

'Tom's my ex-brother-in-law,' she said, trying to sound diffident. As if it was of no moment. 'That's why I came here in the first place, to help him while he was ill. But I don't want to work with him.'

Adam nodded and then looked studiously down at Tasha's notes. 'And your baby's father?' he said gently. 'Would he be on the scene?'

And there was no use hiding it. If things went to plan, this man would be delivering her baby, and Tom had made it quite clear he wanted to be there for her.

'Tom's the father.'

She waited for shock. She waited for condemnation but none came. Instead, Adam searched her face with concern. He was a man in his sixties, with the air of a doctor who'd seen it all, and was surprised by nothing. 'I know Tom well,' he said at last. 'I suspect he'll make an excellent father, if he's involved.'

'That's what he wants,' she admitted. 'I'm not sure it's what I want. This pregnancy…wasn't exactly planned.'

He shook his head in mock disgust. 'Really? I have no idea what they teach medical students these days, but I'm thinking I need to write to the people who trained you.' There was another silence while who knew what went through the obstetrician's head, but finally he beamed. 'Well, well,' he said. 'Planned or not, you should make this work. You and Tom… Cray Point and Summer Bay aren't so far apart. Barring complications, you can deliver here in Summer Bay hospital. We're small but we're good. You'll find this a supportive practice and with Tom supporting you as well…'

'I don't need his support.'

'There's no one I'd rather have as my support person,' Adam said gently. 'As a doctor, Tom

Blake is one in a million. I have no idea what he'd be like as a partner or a father but I'm guessing good.' And then he shook his head. 'But that's none of my business, so all I'll say is welcome to Summer Bay, Dr Raymond. We'll be very happy to have you on board.'

She still had a week to go at Cray Point. She drove back feeling faintly ill but it wasn't morning sickness this time.

Why was everyone telling her what a great guy Tom was? Why did she feel that everyone was seeing something she couldn't see?

Or was it the other way round? Was it that she was seeing—fearing?—something that wasn't there?

Tom wasn't pressing her. After that one night on the back steps with the cat and the pregnancy stick he seemed to have retired into the background. He let her be.

She still saw him in morning surgery but she'd stopped going to rehab with him. As far as she knew he was back to setting candles and flowers on the veranda.

'You really are a coward.' She said it out loud as she drove back along the coast road but there wasn't anything she could do about it. Her fear was too deeply ingrained.

'I love him,' she said out loud, but admitting it made the knot of fear tug even tighter.

'So I'm a coward,' she told herself. 'I can't take a chance, but to do anything else seemed impossible.'

Tom wouldn't pressure her. He'd be there for her baby and that was lovely. Sort of.

If she only had the courage...

'I don't,' she whispered. 'And there's not a thing I can do about it.'

Three more days.

Hilda and her father were due back on Tuesday. Tom still wasn't operating at a hundred percent but he was coping.

There was a nice little hospital apartment waiting for her at Summer Bay.

She'd done what she'd come for. She needed to move on.

With baby.

But she was trying very hard not to think of baby. It was so early. She could still miscarry. Anything could happen.

'You're a wound-up ball of emotion,' Rhonda

told her. 'Why not relax, dear? Tom wants to take over. Why not let him? Enjoy your last weekend. You could even go surfing. Tom reckons he'll be back in the surf any day now.'

'All the more reason for me not to relax,' she snapped, and then she recovered and apologised.

What was happening to her? She was turning into a grouch.

Maybe that's what terror did.

She spent Saturday morning thinking about packing but most of the time she sat and stared out the window to the bay beyond. She needed to organise her own car. She needed to organise her new home, to move on, but she seemed trapped in a fog of lethargy.

'It'll be fine,' she told herself. 'I have a great new job. I have a neat apartment and I can choose a lovely new car. I'll…'

And then she paused because she couldn't think past that.

I'll what?

Carry this baby to term? Have a safe delivery? Live happily every after?

Without Tom.

Without courage.

She was feeling so bleak she was close to tears,

but tears were stupid. When the phone rang she was so desperate for distraction she almost ran to it, but Rhonda beat her. And as Tasha reached the hall she saw Rhonda's face lose colour.

'It's Tom,' Rhonda said, putting the phone down, and the look on her face scared Tasha to the bone.

'Another bleed?' Please, God, not another bleed.

'Tasha, no, sorry. I've scared you more than Karen's just scared me. No, Tom's okay.'

'Karen?'

'You know Karen, our taxi driver. She's rung to say three lads have been bird-nesting on the cliffs above the bluff. Alex, James and Rowan. Of course, those three again! Of all the idiots... It's loose shale and a sheer drop to the rocks and surf below. Stupid, stupid kids. It was Rowan who almost killed himself last time and came close to killing Tom with him. Rowan only suffered bruises but Tom ended up with a cerebral bleed. Now it's James at the bottom of the cliff, and Tom's saying he's climbing down to help him. With his weak leg and arm. Karen says can we come because someone's got to stop him, but the lad's in trouble and Tom says he's going anyway.'

* * *

It should take ten minutes to get from Rhonda's to the bluff but Rhonda covered it in what seemed two, driving like someone in a James Bond movie and swearing all the time.

'Idiot, idiot, idiot,' she kept muttering. 'He thinks he has to save the world. Where would this town be without him, and he risks it all for one stupid kid? Again.'

'Do we know how badly James is hurt?' Tasha asked in a small voice as Rhonda took the next turn on two wheels. Tasha hardly noticed.

'Broken leg. Pete Simmonds has gone down—they called him first because he's a climber. An abseiler. He went down, risking himself, but he says there's hardly room on the ledge for one. Apparently he's anchored James and come up again to let a medic go down. Karen says there's something urgent needs doing with James's leg that can't wait for the rescue chopper. So Tom's saying he's going down and Pete's just realised how weak Tom's leg is and Karen says you need to talk sense into him.'

Talk sense into a Blake boy? She didn't think so but Rhonda swung the car off the road onto the bluff and skidded to a halt beside the Cray Point fire truck, and Tasha was left with no choice but to try.

Tom was already kitted up. He was wearing a harness. He was kneeling by the cliff edge, sorting gear into a backpack, looking grim. He didn't look up as Tasha approached. He didn't see her until she put her hand on her shoulder and held. Hard.

'What do you think you're doing?' she asked, and she was a bit stunned by how her voice came out. She sounded angry.

But he kept right on packing. 'I need to go down,' he told her. 'James has a compound leg fracture. Pete says it's bent back at an impossible angle and the foot's cold to the touch. He's conscious, ten feet above the surf. The rescue chopper's caught up with an overturned boat and might be an hour. I'm going down now.'

'Have you abseiled this type of cliff before?'

'Pete's told me how.'

'So that's a no?'

'I can do it.'

'With a gammy leg and a gammy arm.'

'There's no choice and you know it.' Still he didn't look up. 'If I don't go down, he loses his leg. He might die.'

He was moving morphine ampules from his bag into the backpack. She stooped, took the ampoules from him and put them in herself.

'Just pack the light stuff,' she said. 'You can lower saline, oxygen, anything heavy I need when I'm down there. I'll need a thinner loop line attached as well so we can guide stuff down.' She looked up at a man who must be Pete—he was big, burly and carrying a coil of business-like rope. 'Can we organise that?'

'Sure, Doc,' Pete said with an uneasy glance at Tom. 'I'm so sorry I can't do stuff myself but I never learned any first aid. Blood makes me want to pass out and the last thing the kid needs down there is me unconscious on top of him.' He hesitated. 'So you reckon you're going down instead of Tom?'

'Of course I am.'

Tom sat back on his heels and stared.

'Of course you're not. I can do this.'

'You might be able to,' she said, meeting his gaze square on, 'if you're lucky. But you have no climbing skills and you still have left-sided weakness. Pete, what are the odds on a first-time climber making it?'

'I don't like it,' Pete said. 'It's loose shale. You

can't depend on footholds. The kids were damned fools to be here. It'll take skill.'

'I have skill,' she said evenly, and then both men were staring at her.

'You,' Tom said, as if she'd suddenly grown two heads.

'It's called trying to keep up with Paul,' she said. 'He wanted to climb things, and for a while I tried to go with him.' She managed a smile. 'I gave up in the end—Paul was never happy unless the climb was dangerous and it turned out he didn't want me with him anyway—but I learned from good people and I've climbed places more difficult than this. Take off the harness, Tom. This is my call.'

'It's dangerous,' Tom said.

'But you were going down.'

'I'm not pregnant,' he retorted.

And suddenly she grinned. Suddenly it seemed like she was back in her emergency ward in London, arguing responsibility with a macho colleague. Equal rights for women had come a long way in medicine but there were still male doctors with a deep-seated belief in their own superiority.

She'd learned to bypass them with humour, no matter how grim the situation. Now she simply reached out and tugged Tom's harness. She took one shoulder, Pete took the other and the harness was removed from Tom before he could react.

'You're right, I'm pregnant and you're not,' she agreed equitably. 'At least I hope you're not. But I don't exactly have a bulge big enough to get bumped. Next objection, Dr Blake?'

'You can't. Hell, Tasha… I'll go nuts if you go down there.'

'Because?'

'It's dangerous.'

'You've already said that. So you'd rather I sat up here and thought the same about you.'

'Yes!'

She smiled again, then looked at the people clustered around them. 'Okay, let's make this democratic. Rhonda, Pete, Karen, we need to vote. On this side of the argument I give you an experienced emergency medicine specialist with solid abseiling skills. I've done much harder climbs than this. I'm fit and I'm prepared. I'll admit I'm also in the very early stages of pregnancy but I have no side effects and that shouldn't make a difference at all.'

'But that's my baby,' Tom groaned, while the onlookers' collective jaws dropped.

'That makes a difference how?' Tasha asked serenely. 'It seems Pollywig's about to have an adventure. You taught me with Emily to introduce my baby to life early. So… Pete, Karen, Rhonda, on the other side of the equation we have Tom, a skilled doctor admittedly, but with no experience in this sort of climbing and residual left-sided weakness. We need to vote. Now.'

But there was no voting to be done. Pete was clipping her harness on, and after a moment's loaded silence Tom finished loading the bag. His face was drawn, his mouth grim.

He rose and helped her on with the backpack. 'You dare fall…'

'I don't dare anything,' she told him, taking the backpack and meeting his gaze square on. 'It's the Blake boys who dare. I'm using my skill set. There's a difference.'

'I shouldn't let you.'

'Sense, Tom, instead of bravado. Who's the most sensible candidate for the job?'

He closed his eyes and when he opened them again she knew he agreed. He still looked grim but he also looked resigned.

'I'm with you every inch of the way.'

'I know.'

And then he smiled, a weary smile that said he was hating what was happening but he knew it was inevitable. Then he took her shoulders and tugged her forward and kissed her.

It was a fast kiss, as circumstances dictated it must be, but it packed a punch. It was hard and strong and an affirmation of worry, of fear. Of love?

And there was also something else. When he pulled away she saw an expression that could only be described as pride. 'You're one amazing woman, Tasha Raymond,' he told her.

'I'm a doctor doing her job,' she told him, and only she knew just how much she wanted to sink back into his arms. But there was work to be done. 'Let's get me down there.'

She'd sounded confident when she'd talked her way into this job. In truth, she was a long way from confident. Climbs could be graded in difficulty and this was high on the scale. The shale and the lack of footholds, the knowledge that her feet could dislodge rock that could fall to the boy below, the steepness of the slope and the roar of the surf...they combined to make a climb where she had to use every one of her skills to keep herself safe.

Pete must have known but he hadn't said, she thought as she manoeuvred herself down the cliff, and she thought Pete would probably prefer it was her risking her neck rather than Tom. Because Tom was the town's doctor and the town loved Tom.

As she loved Tom. His image stayed with her, as did the look on his face as she disappeared over the edge of the cliff. There wasn't a person there who didn't look frightened, but Tom...

He looked haggard and she hated that he looked like that.

Every trace of her concentration was taken with climbing, keeping herself steady, not disturbing the shale, but deep within she was conscious of an almost subconscious undercurrent of thought.

Tom was almost as terrified for her as she'd once been terrified for Emily. But he'd let her go. He'd conceded she had the skills and he'd stepped aside, even if it had almost killed him.

She was suddenly thinking of Rhonda's words.

'It was Rowan nearly killed himself last time and nearly killed Tom with him. Rowan ended

up only with bruises but Tom ended up with a cerebral bleed.'

And suddenly she was thinking of the meaning behind Rhonda's words. Maybe she hadn't asked enough questions. She'd assumed Tom had been injured doing his own reckless, Blake boy thing, but maybe he hadn't. Maybe he'd been in the position she was in now, where he was the one with the skills. He'd been able to surf so he'd been the one to rescue Rowan.

Smashing his head might not have been because of reckless behaviour. It might not have been no more reckless than what she was doing now.

She'd categorised him as a Blake boy. A womaniser. A testosterone-driven risk-taker.

Maybe she'd been wrong.

She was two-thirds of the way down now, closer to the boy at the bottom than she was to Tom, but suddenly she felt so close to Tom it was as if he was physically beside her.

It had taken courage to let her go. She knew it had. How much harder to stand aside and let the one you love take the risks...

She was taking a risk now, she acknowledged

as she fought to keep herself steady, fought to stop herself spinning and hitting the shale.

How much greater a risk was falling for Tom?

How much greater a risk than falling was loving someone who loved her?

And then she found herself thinking of Iris and Ron and their appalling relationship, and then back to her own dreadful marriage. And suddenly she was swinging on a rope half way down a cliff, thinking she must have had rocks in her head until now.

'Because Tom's been my very best friend for almost two years,' she whispered. 'So how can I possibly compare? I think I must have been a little bit mad.'

He was going quietly crazy.

Pete was doing all the work, feeding out line, keeping in radio contact to give advice, keeping Tasha as safe as he could, so for the moment there was nothing Tom could do.

Pete's face was grim. He knew the risks. He knew what Tasha was being asked to do.

James's parents were clinging to each other. James's friends were huddled against their parents, turned from defiant teens to children again, wanting comfort.

'We were just trying to reach the easy nests from the top,' Rowan was muttering, and his dad gave him a clout across the shoulders and then hugged him.

That was pretty much how Tom was feeling. Anger and love. Anger that Tasha should be in this position. Anger that she'd even offered to go. Fury and frustration that he'd had to accept that offer.

Pride and love that she was down there, working to save a life.

Tasha. The woman he loved with all his heart.

He'd never thought he could feel like this.

His father and his half-brother had walked out on women they'd sworn to love, betraying them in the worst possible way.

'They didn't really love.' He said it out loud, not caring who heard, and suddenly Rhonda was beside him, putting her hand in his.

'She'll be okay.'

'You don't know that.'

'We all love her,' Rhonda said. 'And she's amazing. You know that, too. All she has to do is climb down a few more feet, straighten one leg and wait for the chopper. What's hard about that?'

But her hand tightened convulsively in his as she spoke and he glanced down at her and saw his fear reflected on her face.

We all love her.

Cray Point had taken her to their hearts. He'd taken her to his heart.

He wanted her.

'Dear God, let her be safe.' He'd wanted her for himself but it didn't matter. He'd barter everything if she could be okay. She could go and live in Summer Bay. She could go back to England if she wanted.

Just let her live.

She made it.

James was huddled in a ball of fear and pain and hardly acknowledged her arrival. Apart from a brief murmur, a touch of reassurance, the first few moments had to be taken with finding herself safe footholds and attaching anchors. There was practically no room. How James had fallen onto what looked like the only outcrop that could hold him was a miracle.

Pete had anchored James as best he could, but

he'd also placed a harness on the boy's shoulders and attached a rope. He'd taken the other end back up to the top when he'd left.

That was worst-case scenario, Tasha knew. That was in case the ledge crumbled or James fell. Anchors were only as solid as the cliff face they were attached to.

That was the reason she stayed in her harness now and wouldn't release the tension of the rope from above. It was her link to safety.

To Tom.

James was huddled hard against the cliff, as far from the edge as it was possible to be—which meant there was about eight inches between his back and the fall to the waves below. He stirred as she arrived but he didn't turn to look at her.

She had to balance on the edge of the ledge to examine him, fighting an instinctive urge to cling to the cliff itself.

'James, you know me,' she told him, bending close so he could hear her over the sound of the surf. 'Doc. Tasha. I saw you when you had a sore throat last month.'

'T-Tom,' James groaned. 'Where's Tom?'

'Up the top of the cliff, where you should be.' She was doing a fast visual assessment. The boy was scratched and bleeding from multiple lacerations. He must have hit shale all the way down. His clothing was ripped and bloodstained. He had a deep cut above his left eye but it was already congealing.

She felt his pulse. It was steady and strong, which was a small reassurance. If he had internal bleeding he'd be in shock by now. She felt his ribs, his abdomen and found nothing obvious. He was conscious, and the kids had said that he'd called out to them as he'd landed, so a head injury was unlikely.

But his leg was twisted at an impossible angle.

She touched the skin at his ankle and winced. Pete was right. His foot was blue and bloodless and cool. This was a compound fracture with compromised blood supply. The tiny amount of blood getting through wasn't enough to keep the foot alive.

He had no massive haematoma or obvious bleed. That meant the vein was probably intact but kinked like a garden hose.

If he wasn't to lose his foot, she had to straighten the leg.

Help.

She needed a theatre. She needed an orthopaedic surgeon, an anaesthetist and a full complement of theatre staff.

'Tasha?'

The voice in her headphones was Tom's and it steadied her. She took a deep breath and answered, one doctor to another.

'I'm down. James is conscious but in a lot of pain. I'm about to give him something to ease it. Five milligrams of morphine intravenously?'

'Right,' Tom said, and it helped to hear him agree. She knew she was right, but saying it out loud settled her. It was as if she had a colleague beside her.

She did have a colleague beside her. Tom was with her every inch of the way.

'James, I'm giving you a shot of something that'll dull the pain,' she told him. 'It won't stop it completely but it'll help.' Then she spoke directly into the speaker attached to her headphones. 'Fractured leg with almost nil blood supply to the foot. Tom, work with me. I need anaesthetist advice.'

'Give me a moment.'

'Thank you,' she said, knowing he'd guessed, grateful that she didn't have to say out loud that she was afraid the morphine wouldn't be enough, that reduction in such circumstances might send James into shock, that she needed to talk to a specialist. He'd guessed she was afraid.

She injected morphine. She washed the worst of the grime from James's face. She worried about how long that leg could stay viable.

And then Tom was speaking again.

'The best option's methoxyflurane,' he told her. 'It's a rapid, short-term analgesic using a portable inhaler and it's in a pack at the base of your backpack. Do you know it?'

'I've heard of it,' she said cautiously. 'I haven't used it.'

'It's mostly used by paramedics and people like me who operate outside the confines of a major hospital. We use it when we need to do acute procedures fast without an anaesthetist, or for high-dose pain relief during transfer. Relief begins after six to eight breaths. As long as James is haemodynamically stable...'

'He is.'

'Then we can use it. Can I talk to him?'

'Sure.' She tugged off her earpieces and put one on James. Then she unashamedly stooped and held the other a little way back so she could listen.

'James, this is Tom. How's it going?'

'B-Bloody,' James managed, but Tasha could tell by his face that even this minimal contact with a doctor he trusted was a reassurance.

'Tasha says you've busted your leg. Idiot,' Tom said, but he sounded almost cheerful, business-like, as if this was little more than a scratch that had to be disinfected. 'She's given you some morphine, which will make you nice and dopey, but the problem is that your leg's a bit bent and the blood's not getting through to the foot.'

'I can't…see.'

'Nor would you want to,' Tom said. 'Bent legs aren't pretty. So Tasha's going to straighten it. She needs to do that before there's long-term damage to your foot, so unless you want to limp for life you'll need to put up with what she does. Sorry, mate, but it's going to hurt. But not for long. Tasha's good, she's fast and we'll get the leg straight and you up the cliff before you know it.'

'I don't want to be here.'

'Yeah, well, you fell down,' Tom said unsympathetically. 'But we're getting the chopper to lift you up. Your mum and dad are up here, ready to give you a good telling-off for bird-nesting in such a dumb place, but they want to give you a hug first. But first your foot. To ease the pain you need to breathe in through the inhaler Tasha gives you. After six to eight breaths the relief will kick in. What Tasha does will hurt but it's just a momentary thing while she sets your leg in position. If you keep breathing through the mask, concentrating on breathing and not the pain, it'll settle. Would you like me to keep talking as she works?'

'Y-yes.'

'Then let's go for it,' Tom said. 'Tasha?'

How did he know she was listening? 'Yes?'

'Go for it, love,' he told her. 'You can do this. I'm with you both.'

She needed X-rays. She needed her patient under a general anaesthetic. She needed a nice clean hospital, and space to work. And an anaesthetic strong enough to hold the pain at bay so she could manoeuvre the fracture slowly, figuring out the best way to re-establish blood supply.

She had none of those things and Tom could only guess at the stress she was under. Pete had taken photos of the smashed leg on his phone before he'd come back up the cliff. The photos were not great quality but Tom could see splintered bone, a mess, a nightmare to try to straighten in these circumstances.

He wanted to tell Tasha not to beat herself up if she failed. He wanted to tell her he expected her to fail, that what she was doing was a long shot.

He couldn't, though, because she'd put the earphones onto James and his role now was to keep James calm so Tasha could work. As well as that, James's parents were within earshot, hanging on his every word.

He could say nothing at all.

She'd told Tom she could.

She had no choice.

It was incredibly difficult to balance on the tiny amount of ledge space she had. The rope attached to her harness was still taut, carefully played so that as she moved it was pulled out and reined in. She wasn't alone. She had Pete holding her harness.

She also had Tom talking to James while James breathed through the mask. It was almost as if Tom was playing the role of anaesthetist.

She had a whole clifftop of people with her every step of the way.

It takes a village to raise a child. Where had

that line come from? She couldn't remember, but there was a village at the top of the cliff. A village who cared.

She'd worked in emergency wards for almost all of her professional life. She'd been surrounded by a team.

Now she should feel isolated, afraid, but strangely she didn't. Her team—her village— was a little distant but it was still there. And Tom was with her. He was at the top of the cliff. He was talking to James but he was still with her.

He was her rock in all this. Tom.

Despite the circumstances, she forced herself to take her time, to think clearly about the way she'd do this. She knew that she had a tiny window to get the vein unkinked. The anaesthetic couldn't mask such pain completely. After a first attempt James would react, his body would freeze and she'd be lucky if she could get near him for a second try.

But for now he seemed almost relaxed. He was trying out the inhaler, breathing steadily, listening to Tom.

She cut the last of his shredded pants away from his leg and spent a little time familiarising herself with every inch of the fractured limb.

The tibia and fibula were both broken. She could see the breaks. They'd been smashed hard across, splintering.

She could feel a pulse above the break but not below. There was little blood getting through.

She sat and looked for as long as she needed to steady herself, to figure how she should hold the leg, how she should pull.

'Tom says how's it going?' James asked in a fuzzy voice, and she knew the anaesthetic was now as strong as it could be.

'Tell Tom we're set to go,' she told him, and placed her hands firmly—confidently?—where she needed them. 'Tell Tom to stay tuned; your leg's about to be fixed.'

'Tasha says we're ready to go,' James whispered between breaths, and Tom felt ill. He wanted to be there. He needed to be there.

'It'll hurt,' he warned the boy. 'But only for a moment. Hang on in there, mate, and whatever you do, don't move. Can you do that?'

'Y-yeah.'

'I know you can. We're all with you. Tell Tasha that, too.'

And then he listened as James murmured to Tasha. Then:

'She says she knows,' James whispered. 'She says I gotta lie still and think of playing footy next year. She says if I lie still she'll come and barrack for me.'

'I bet she will,' Tom said unsteadily. 'And I'll come, too. But for now just breathe through the inhaler. Deep breaths...'

And then James screamed.

Seconds felt like hours. She still held James's leg firmly, so he couldn't react by hauling back, twisting, possibly undoing what she'd hoped she'd done.

She could hear the faint sound of Tom's voice speaking to James in the background. He was the one talking James down from the peak of pain.

He had to be. Her hands held James's leg and every trace of her concentration was on the foot below the break. She was holding the leg steady and she was pleading. Please...

And when it came she could hardly believe it. A trace of colour...

I'm imagining it, she told herself, but a moment

later she knew she wasn't. She dared to touch his ankle and she felt...a pulse.

'Oh, James,' she said weakly, and then she forced herself to speak more strongly because even though she felt weak at the knees James had to see her as physician in charge. 'Well done, you. Well done, us. Blood's getting through to your foot. You're going to be okay.'

'Y-you hear?' James managed, and she knew he was speaking to Tom.

And then James managed a wan smile.

'Tom says to tell you you're a bloody hero,' he told her. 'He says he knows Mum won't let me swear but that's what you are. But, strewth, Doc, that hurt.'

The chopper arrived twenty minutes later. It was a complex operation, getting James onto a cradle with his leg firmly fixed, securing him, then swinging him up to the top of the cliff.

For a while Tasha was left sitting by herself on the ledge, and almost as soon as the cradle swung outwards she started to shake.

When they finally came for her, they had to treat her as a patient. She was shaking too much to be of any assistance.

'Got you, sweetheart,' the cheerful paramedic said as he harnessed himself to her. They swung off the ledge and hung momentarily over the ocean. 'You're safe.'

She didn't feel safe. She didn't feel safe until she was lowered onto solid ground on the clifftop.

Until she was gathered into Tom's arms and held.

Until she was home.

CHAPTER ELEVEN

TOM WENT WITH the chopper to Melbourne. The paramedic in charge accepted Tom's offer with relief.

'I'll say yes, mate,' he told him. 'You guys have done brilliantly, getting that blood supply working, and I don't want it blocking again on my watch. If you're in the back with him we have more chance of doing something if it blocks again.'

So Tom gave Tasha a hard, swift hug and followed James into the chopper.

'Look after her, Rhonda,' he ordered, and Rhonda took over the Tasha-hugging and nodded.

'She'll be looked after. Every single person in this town will be offering to make her cups of tea but I'm first.'

'I wouldn't mind a whisky,' Tasha told her, but managed a smile. 'But tea will be great. I'll stay on duty.'

'I know you will,' Tom said, the warmth in his

smile a caress all by itself, and then he swung himself into the helicopter, the engine roared into full power and he was gone.

She went home with Rhonda, who bullied her into a bath, then made her eat, then left her to relax.

Tasha knew where she needed to be. She walked slowly up to the headland, to the cemetery, to a tiny grave. Who knew how long she sat there? She didn't know. All she knew was that the tumult that had been in her head, seemingly since the time she'd learned of Paul's betrayal, had somehow settled.

Tonight there were things that needed to be said. She might as well say them first to her daughter.

'Tom's right,' she told her. 'He's not a Blake boy. He's just Tom.' And then she thought about her words and decided they needed changing.

'But he's not *just* Tom,' she said. 'He's my Tom and I love him. And maybe it's time I realised what brave really is.'

Once the chopper had landed at The Melbourne, once a specialist medical team had wheeled into motion and once James's mum and dad were assured James was in the best possible care, Tom was free to leave. There was a bus in the morning. He could get a bed at the hospital and Tasha was in Cray Point tonight to cope with any emergencies. There was no need to hurry back. Regardless, he hired a car. What was the point of finally being permitted to drive again if he didn't? He headed home.

To Tasha?

He needed to stop that train of thought, he told himself as he drove. Tasha was leaving. Living in Summer Bay, he'd see her often, as a friend, as the mother of his child, but for now he needed to back off and let her be.

But he wanted to see her, and he wanted to see her *now*.

What excuse did he have? None, he thought, but as he drove into Cray Point it was all he could do not to turn towards Rhonda's.

He had no reason to take the turn. Tasha would know James was safe. Rhonda had been on the phone demanding frequent updates, and he knew she'd have passed them on to the town.

Tasha would know everything she needed to know.

Except how much she was loved?

She knew that, too, he told himself, but it didn't make any difference. She didn't want him.

What a joke. He'd finally met a woman he wanted to share the rest of his life with, and she had the same mistrust of commitment he'd spent his life with.

He turned the last bend towards home, feeling black.

The lights were on at his place. All the lights.

He pulled to a halt under the veranda and saw the table was set outside. A mass of candles formed a centrepiece to the table. A huge spray of wildflowers trailed under the candlelight.

Tasha was in the doorway.

His breath caught in his throat. She was wearing a sliver of a shimmering, silver dress, a dress that accentuated every luscious curve. Her curls were loose around her shoulders and her face looked almost luminescent.

She was smiling out at him as his car drew to a halt and he'd never seen anyone look more beautiful.

'Hi,' she called, and heaven knew the effort it cost to get his voice to work to call back.

'Hi.' He climbed from the car and glanced at the table, the crystal, the silver cutlery, the best dinner set, his grandmother's finest stuff he never used even for his more elaborate dinners. 'You're expecting company?'

'I'm expecting you.' She waved an airy hand towards the table. 'Rhonda said you were on your way back. Have I forgotten anything?'

He made his way cautiously up the veranda steps, feeling it behoved a man to be cautious. The look of her... He'd only ever seen her in casual and work clothes. This dress... He wanted to put his hands on her waist and hold.

She was stunning.

He was stunned.

'This looks a bit overkill for my usual dinners,' he said cautiously, and she smiled, a smile that lit her whole face.

'It's not a usual dinner,' she told him. 'Your seduction settings are for your trail of assorted women...'

'I do not have a trail...'

'You do have a trail,' she told him, lovingly though, as if she finally understood him, as if she wanted him just the way he was. 'They're very assorted. Rhonda tells me you've had fun and the women you've dined here have had fun as well. So I thought...maybe we could have fun, too.'

'You're offering to be…a part of my trail?'

She shook her head. She still stood in the doorway and he hadn't made it further than the top step. There seemed a vast distance. A distance he wasn't sure he could cross.

'Not a part of your trail,' she said softly, and for the first time she sounded a bit unsure. As if it was taking courage to say what she had to say. 'The end of your trail. And even though my trail hasn't been candles and flowers, I'm hoping it's the end of my trail, too. If you want me.'

The words took his breath away. He should step forward and sweep her into his arms right now, but somehow he forced himself to stay where he was. There were things he needed to sort. There were things he needed to know.

'You don't trust me,' he said at last.

'Past tense. That's my blindness and I'm sorry.' She wasn't moving either. She was leaning against the doorjamb as if she needed its support. 'I've never been very brave, you see.'

'I don't understand.'

She shrugged and tried for a smile that didn't quite come off. 'My parents were adventurers,' she told him. They were both in the army, and they put their hands up for any exciting conflict going. There were dramas all through my childhood—one or the other of them was always getting injured. That was practically the only time I saw them, when they were recuperating. When I grew up I thought I'd be a doctor. It was a nice, safe profession, filled with good, dependable people.

'Only I must have had some of my parents' drive for adventure because I joined Médicins Sans Frontières and I met Paul. I fell for him. Heaven help me, I even tried to keep up with him. There were so many attempts at brave there, and every one of them was a disaster. After Paul I went back to being safe but then I thought I'd really like a baby. That felt huge. It felt totally unsafe but I did it anyway. My final brave.'

'And then Emily died,' he said softly, and she closed her eyes for a moment.

'Yes,' she whispered. 'And I thought that's the end. But there was a niggle that had me wanting another baby. Aching for another baby. Maybe I could summon enough courage to try one more time. But then…then I fell in love with you and I thought how like Paul you were. And I realised that I couldn't trust myself. The whole idea of a baby, of a future seemed to disintegrate and I thought, I don't have enough courage for anything.'

'Tasha, you're the bravest—'

But she shook her head. 'Wait. Please.' She took a deep breath and forced herself to go on. 'Tom, brave or not, I've finally figured…today I figured… I've had the definition wrong. Somehow in my muddle of a mind I equated brave with stupid. I thought you were like my parents. Like Paul. Like your dad. Taking risks for risks' sake.'

'It's not like that.'

'I know it's not,' she whispered. 'This morning when I thought you were climbing down the cliff, I was as terrified as I'd ever been. There you go, being brave again. Being stupid. And then Rhonda told me about your surfing accident. You went onto the reef deliberately to save Rowan. And on the cliff today… If you'd been Paul, there'd have been no way you'd have let me go down in your stead. So I went there expecting to be terrified while you did your foolhardy thing. Instead, you accepted facts, you weighed risks and you let me go.'

'And I was terrified instead.'

'I know you were,' she whispered. 'And that's when I realised there's brave and brave. Brave isn't always about putting your life on the line. Brave's also about watching from the sidelines, letting the man you love take the risks he has to take, knowing he'll do the same for you.' She took a deep breath. 'Brave is also saying what's past is past and shouldn't affect the future. Brave might also be about saying I want a family. I want Pollywig to have a dad and I want to love her dad. And… And brave's saying I do love you.'

She stopped and the whole world seemed to hold its breath. Tom didn't speak. He couldn't. He couldn't begin to understand the surge of emotion in his chest. He could hardly begin to hope.

'Tom…' Tasha whispered, and he wanted to go to her but still he couldn't. He held out a hand as if to reach her but his body seemed frozen.

'So I thought I'd leave a proposal for after main course,' she said unsteadily. 'How do they do it in the movies? A ring in the chocolate mousse and then a comedy routine where our hero proposes while our heroine gets her stomach pumped to retrieve her diamond? But I'm not that brave.'

'You're brave enough for anything,' he managed, and finally he got his feet to work, finally he strode forward and took her waist in his hands and drew her to him. 'Love, what are you saying?'

'I'm asking whether this seduction scene has finally worked like it's supposed to,' she whispered, her voice muffled now against his chest. But then she pulled back. He held her at arm's length, gazing down into her gorgeous eyes, and she managed to smile up at him. And all the love in the world was in her eyes.

'I'm saying that finally I get this brave thing,' she whispered. 'And I'm going with it. So, Tom Blake, here's the thing.' She took a deep breath. 'I love you and I want to spend the rest of my life with you. I want to carry your child and I want to share. I want to be brave with you and occasionally I want to be a coward with you. I love you just the way you are, Tom Blake, and I can't wait until after the main course and I don't have a ring anyway so therefore...'

But he wouldn't let her go any further. He put his finger on her lips and shushed her and then he smiled, a smile that felt like it was turning him into a different person. A man who could walk forward from this moment.

'Allow me some pride, my love,' he told her. 'Damn, where's a diamond when you need one?'

He glanced around at the ornate table, at his grandmother's silver napkin rings. He seized one and dropped to his knee.

'Tom...' Tasha was half laughing, half crying.

'Shh,' he told her. 'This is important.' And he took both her hands in his and gazed up at her. 'Tasha Raymond, it's my turn to be brave,' he told her. 'So I'm risking everything here, including the messing up of one heirloom napkin ring set. But what the heck. Tasha, will you do me the honour of becoming my wife?'

And what was a woman to say to that?

There was nothing to say. She dropped to her knees as well. He put the crazy, too-big ring on her finger and it almost fitted her fist. He smiled down at it and then he smiled at her.

He drew her into his arms and kissed her.

Tasha had gone to some trouble with the dinner. She'd made a casserole, with expensive steak and wine.

The casserole burned, for taking the casserole from the oven when the timer went meant risking breaking the moment, and who were Tasha and Tom to take risks?

They weren't risk-takers.

They were very safe indeed.

* * *

There was no hospital at Cray Point. There was one at Summer Bay, though. With Adam Myers in charge, it had good obstetric care, so with all the scans showing normal, Tom and Tasha decided that's where their daughter would be born.

One beautiful autumn day Tasha went into natural labour.

For some reason Tasha had woken thinking the weeds had to be dealt with *immediately.* Tom had his way first, though, and they'd had a gentle morning's surf.

Tom had taught Tasha to surf on their honeymoon, but now it was as much as she could do to lie in the shallows and let the sun play on her bump. But that had felt pretty good.

They'd come home. She'd had a nap while Tom had started on the weeds and then she'd joined him. There were no medical imperatives. The soil was damp and still warm, so weeding was easy. Tasha finally confessed her contractions to Tom but she didn't want to stop.

'Let's get this bed done first,' she told him. 'I fancy sweet peas and cornflowers in spring.'

So—reluctantly on Tom's part—they weeded

on, and Tasha grew quieter but more and more adamant that she wanted to stay where she was.

Finally she straightened and stretched and winced and gave in to what her body was telling her. 'Maybe it's time to go,' she admitted.

Tom needed no second telling. He'd packed the car the moment Tasha had admitted to her first contraction, and had taken Rambo, their six-month-old cocker spaniel, to Iris for safekeeping. Keeping on weeding had been a superhuman effort on his part.

'We'll wait until the contractions are ten minutes apart and regular before we head for hospital,' Tasha had reminded him.

How many times had he told his patients that? Yet when it was his own he wanted to break every rule in the book.

But finally she was agreeing. She went inside to wash—and he found her at the sink, bent double with the force of the next contraction.

Tom practically carried her to the car, but as he helped her in, another contraction hit.

'That's less than two minutes,' he said blankly.

'I told you it was time,' Tasha managed when she could catch her breath. She was trying to sound serene but not quite managing it.

He practically ran to the driver's side. As he hit the ignition Tasha moaned with yet another contraction.

'You've got to be kidding!' The contractions seemed to be rolling into one.

'It's okay,' she muttered. 'There's plenty...of time.'

'Tasha...'

'Just drive.'

He turned out of the driveway, up along the headland towards the road to Summer Bay but he knew before he'd gone five hundred yards that they weren't going to make it.

'Um...' Tasha was arching back, moaning. 'Oh, Tom... Oh, whoops... I can feel... Tom, sorry, I might have mistimed... I thought we might...' She moaned through another contraction and then: 'Tom, stop!'

They were high on the headland. The land here sloped gently down to the sea in a vast sweep of lush autumnal green pasture. The view was breathtaking. How many times had they walked up here to lay flowers on Emily's grave, or to sit and talk, or simply be?

It was their favourite place in the world.

'Tom, stop this minute. Stop! *Oh-h-h-h...*'

There was nothing for him to do but pull to a halt.

Their baby was coming.

Help. He had obstetric supplies in the trunk—of course he did—but he didn't want supplies. He wanted a fully equipped hospital, specialist care, someone other than him...

There was no one. The sun was low on the horizon, sending a silver shimmer on the ocean that would soon turn to tangerine. It was late Sunday afternoon and the day trippers had long gone. The road was deserted, and Tasha was unmistakably moving into the second stage of labour.

'I think I need to push,' she said, quite conversationally, and Tom decided to panic. He was feeling as cowardly as he'd ever felt in his life.

'Hey, Tom, we can do this,' Tasha breathed. 'We've been brave before.'

'We take turns, remember?' It was a dumb thing to say but it was all he could think of.

'This time we share.'

He had no choice. He hauled himself together—somehow—grabbed a resus blanket from the trunk and laid it on the lush grass under a stand of gumtrees. He folded his jacket for a pillow.

He rang for the ambulance.

'Sure, Doc.' The paramedic sounded almost as if he'd expected the call. 'We're on our way. Keep us on speaker phone if you're worried. We'll talk you through it if you need us but you know what to do better than us.'

Strangely Tasha looked almost peaceful. The grass was long and soft underneath the blanket. A couple of cows were hanging their heads over the roadside fence, looking on with interest. The surf was a faint hush-hush below them and, now she was settled on her blanket, Tasha was riding each contraction with determination.

In between she seemed almost relaxed.

Tom wasn't.

'We've rehearsed this,' she managed, as the next contraction passed.

'We rehearsed me being up at your end with an obstetrician being at the business end.'

'Tom...'

'Tasha?'

'This is good,' she told him, but then another contraction hit, stronger than those before. Her serenity slipped and he heard the edge of panic. 'Okay. Maybe...maybe this wasn't a good idea,' she whispered. 'I think...I'm losing it.'

What wasn't a good idea? Had she planned this type of birth?

But it was too late to worry about that now. She needed him.

And wasn't that the whole truth? he thought as he gripped her hands while she rode out the next contraction. Tasha needed Tom. Tom needed Tasha.

Family…

And somehow things settled. Somehow the world righted on its axis.

He and Tasha were together and they were about to welcome the next addition to their family. All indications were that this birth was completely normal. What did he have to be brave about?

And finally he moved into medical mode.

'Small breaths,' he told her. 'Let's see if we can take this labour off the boil for a bit. The ambulance should be here soon. Pant.'

Tasha told him where he could put his panting.

'Tasha…'

'Let's…have…our…baby…' she managed. 'Oh…'

And two minutes later a perfect baby girl slithered out into the arms of her waiting father.

Tom sat back on his heels and gazed down in incredulity at the miracle in his arms. A daughter. He and Tasha had a daughter.

'Is she okay?' It was a whisper, a feather breath.

'She's perfect.' And then he caught himself. Skin to skin was almost the first rule of obstetrics. Now their baby was born, he needed to get her onto her mother's breast, and here he was, staring down like an idiot.

At his daughter.

She wasn't crying. She was wide-eyed, as if she was gazing straight at him.

He wanted to weep. Instead, he managed to be a tiny bit professional. He covered his daughter in his sweater and placed her on her Tasha's breast.

And then he forgot for a moment that he was the doctor in charge. This was his wife. This was his daughter. Who could stay professional?

He gathered them both into his arms and he held them as if they were the most precious creatures in the world.

As they were. His wife. His daughter.

'Rosamund?' Tasha whispered. 'After your grandma, right?'

'If that's okay...'

'It's perfect,' Tasha breathed, and her smile

was so cat-that-got-the-cream that he pulled back a little.

'Did you plan this?'

'No,' she whispered. 'Or...I might have hidden a couple of contractions. I sort of wanted...'

To deliver her baby here, in peace, away from the clinical efficiency of the hospital, from anywhere that would have brought back memories of past pain. High on the headland where she could see all the way to the Antarctic. Where she could see the tiny township of Cray Point—their home. Where she could even see the graveyard where Emily had been laid to rest.

He'd never have agreed, but it was too late to protest now, and indeed it was perfect.

They lay on the blanket, Rosamund warmly wrapped, enclosed between her mother and father.

Family.

They lay as the sun slipped further towards the horizon and started losing its warmth.

'We need to move,' Tom told her. 'Love...'

'Maybe we do.' She sighed and she wriggled a bit and found her phone, which was lying by her side. It was still showing a current call. Speaker phone was on.

'Maybe we do,' she said again. 'I think we're ready, guys.' And then she grinned at Tom, a smile that contained cheek as well as joy. 'You think I took a risk?' she said serenely. 'I never would, not with our family. I might be brave, but I'm not stupid.'

And within a minute the ambulance rounded the bend and pulled to a halt. Out of the ambulance came two paramedics, plus Brenda, plus Adam Myers, the Summer Bay obstetrician.

They moved seamlessly into action, a full obstetric team. Leaving Tom gobsmacked.

'You orchestrated this...' he managed.

'I hoped,' Tasha told him, smiling and smiling. Rosamund was sucking contentedly at her breast. Brenda was fussing with warm blankets. Adam was doing something about the placenta but who cared what? 'What's the point of being doctors if we can't have our tribe help us when we need them?' she asked. 'So I talked to Adam and he agreed...'

'I don't usually do home births,' Adam said gruffly. 'But this wasn't exactly a home birth. A birth with an ambulance parked right around the next bend, with all the equipment we could possibly need, with the two of you doctors... We were ready to pull out at a moment's notice if anything went wrong, and if there'd been some other medical emergency needing the ambulance—or even if the weather was bad—we never would have tried it. Tasha agreed to that but we pulled it off.'

Then the gruff obstetrician paused and glanced out over the cliffs to the sea beyond. 'We pulled it off,' he said again, sounding supremely contented. 'Given our time again, my wife and I might even have risked the same thing. Congratulations to you both. And, no, there's no need to thank us,' he said as Tom tried to think of what he could possibly say. 'The planning was fun and isn't that what life's supposed to be? We put up with the grey for the gold, and this is gold. All of us will remember it.'

And then he smiled at them both. 'But the sun's almost down,' he told them. 'There's a chill in the air. It's time to load you all into the ambulance and take you to a nice warm bed. It's time for you to move on to the next part of your lives.

And Tasha looked at Rosamund and smiled and smiled, and Tom looked at his wife and daughter and thought life couldn't be any more perfect than it was right now.

His Tasha. His one true love.

His brave heart, his soul-mate.

'I love you,' he whispered, and he gathered them close. His wife. His daughter. His family. And Tasha lifted her face to be kissed.

'I love you,' she whispered back.

And then they let the world take over as they moved seamlessly into the next stage of their lives.

Together.

* * * * *

If you enjoyed this story, check out these other great reads from Marion Lennox

A CHILD TO OPEN THEIR HEARTS
SAVING MADDIE'S BABY

STEPPING INTO THE PRINCE'S WORLD
HIS CINDERELLA HEIRESS

All available now!

MILLS & BOON®
Large Print Medical

August

Their Meant-to-Be Baby
A Mummy for His Baby
Rafael's One Night Bombshell
Dante's Shock Proposal
A Forever Family for the Army Doc
The Nurse and the Single Dad

Caroline Anderson
Molly Evans
Tina Beckett
Amalie Berlin
Meredith Webber
Dianne Drake

September

Their Secret Royal Baby
Her Hot Highland Doc
His Pregnant Royal Bride
Baby Surprise for the Doctor Prince
Resisting Her Army Doc Rival
A Month to Marry the Midwife

Carol Marinelli
Annie O'Neil
Amy Ruttan
Robin Gianna
Sue MacKay
Fiona McArthur

October

Their One Night Baby
Forbidden to the Playboy Surgeon
A Mother to Make a Family
The Nurse's Baby Secret
The Boss Who Stole Her Heart
Reunited by Their Pregnancy Surprise

Carol Marinelli
Fiona Lowe
Emily Forbes
Janice Lynn
Jennifer Taylor
Louisa Heaton

MILLS & BOON®
Large Print Medical

November

Mummy, Nurse...Duchess?	Kate Hardy
Falling for the Foster Mum	Karin Baine
The Doctor and the Princess	Scarlet Wilson
Miracle for the Neurosurgeon	Lynne Marshall
English Rose for the Sicilian Doc	Annie Claydon
Engaged to the Doctor Sheikh	Meredith Webber

December

Healing the Sheikh's Heart	Annie O'Neil
A Life-Saving Reunion	Alison Roberts
The Surgeon's Cinderella	Susan Carlisle
Saved by Doctor Dreamy	Dianne Drake
Pregnant with the Boss's Baby	Sue MacKay
Reunited with His Runaway Doc	Lucy Clark

January

The Surrogate's Unexpected Miracle	Alison Roberts
Convenient Marriage, Surprise Twins	Amy Ruttan
The Doctor's Secret Son	Janice Lynn
Reforming the Playboy	Karin Baine
Their Double Baby Gift	Louisa Heaton
Saving Baby Amy	Annie Claydon